OTHER YOUNG ADULT TITLES
FROM SMART POP BOOKS

Demigods and Monsters
*Your Favorite Authors on Rick Riordan's Percy Jackson
and the Olympians*

Ender's World
Fresh Perspectives on the SF Classic Ender's Game

Flirtin' with the Monster
Your Favorite Authors on Ellen Hopkins' Crank and Glass

The Girl Who Was on Fire
Your Favorite Authors on Suzanne Collins' Hunger Games Trilogy

Mind-Rain
Your Favorite Authors on Scott Westerfeld's Uglies Series

A New Dawn
Your Favorite Authors on Stephenie Meyer's Twilight Series

Nyx in the House of Night
*Mythology, Folklore, and Religion in the P.C.
and Kristin Cast Vampyre Series*

The Panem Companion
*An Unofficial Guide to Suzanne Collins' Hunger Games, From
Mellark Bakery to Mockingjays*

Shadowhunters and Downworlders
A Mortal Instruments Reader

Through the Wardrobe
Your Favorite Authors on C.S. Lewis' Chronicles of Narnia

DIVERGENT
THINKING

DIVERGENT THINKING

YA AUTHORS ON VERONICA ROTH'S DIVERGENT TRILOGY

EDITED BY LEAH WILSON

POP

AN IMPRINT OF BENBELLA BOOKS, INC.
DALLAS, TEXAS

3 1257 02466 2537

Smart Pop is an imprint of BenBella Books, Inc.
10300 N. Central Expressway, Suite 530 | Dallas, TX 75231
www.benbellabooks.com | www.smartpopbooks.com
Send feedback to feedback@benbellabooks.com

Printed in the United States of America
10 9 8 7 6 5 4 3 2 1

Library of Congress Cataloging-in-Publication Data
Divergent Thinking : YA Authors on Veronica Roth's Divergent Trilogy / edited by Leah Wilson.
    pages cm
   ISBN 978-1-939529-92-3 (paperback) — ISBN 978-1-940363-34-9 (electronic) 1. Roth, Veronica. Divergent series. 2. Young adult fiction, American—History and criticism. I. Wilson, Leah, editor of compilation.
   PS3618.O8633Z58 2014
   813'.6—dc23   2013049188

Copyediting by Brittany Dowdle, Word Cat Editorial Services
Proofreading by Jenny Bridges and Michael Fedison
Text design and composition by Silver Feather Design
Printed by Bang Printing

Distributed by Perseus Distribution | www.perseusdistribution.com
To place orders through Perseus Distribution:
Tel: (800) 343-4499 | Fax: (800) 351-5073
E-mail: orderentry@perseusbooks.com

Significant discounts for bulk sales are available. Please contact Glenn Yeffeth at glenn@benbellabooks.com or (214) 750-3628.

COPYRIGHT ACKNOWLEDGMENTS

"From Factions to Fire Signs" © 2014 by Rosemary Clement-Moore
"Divergent Psychology" © 2014 by Jennifer Lynn Barnes
"Mapping Divergent's Chicago" © 2014 by V. Arrow
"Choices Can Be Made Again" © 2014 by Maria V. Snyder and Jenna Snyder
"Ordinary Acts of Bravery" © 2014 by Elizabeth Norris
"Fear and the Dauntless Girl" © 2014 by Blythe Woolston
"They Injure Each Other in the Same Way" © 2014 by Mary Borsellino
"Secrets and Lies" © 2014 by Debra Driza
"Bureau versus Rebels: Which Is Worse?" © 2014 by Dan Krokos
"Factions: The Good, the Bad, and the Ugly" © 2014 by Julia Karr
"The Downfall of Dauntless" © 2014 by Janine K. Spendlove
"Emergent" © 2014 by Elizabeth Gatland
Images © 2014 by Risa Rodil, RisaRodil.com

Faction and Chicago location icons © 2014 by Risa Rodil, RisaRodil.com

Water Tower Place photograph courtesy Jrissman, http://en.wikipedia.
org/wiki/File:WaterTowerPlaceMall.JPG

Harold Washington Library photograph courtesy Beyond My Ken,
http://en.wikipedia.org/wiki/File:Harold_Washington_Library_
southwest_owl.jpg

Flamingo photograph courtesy Richie Diesterheft, http://www.flickr.
com/photos/puroticorico/

CONTENTS

INTRODUCTION

A lot of people have called the Divergent trilogy "the next Hunger Games." It's a fair comparison in some ways: they're both science-fiction dystopias with prickly, complex heroines. They've both left millions of readers thinking about them long after reading their final pages (even if—or maybe in part because—their endings were a little controversial). And, like many other dystopias, they both wrestle with the idea of control and how we resist it.

But where the Hunger Games engages with control on a societal level, the Divergent trilogy is more focused on the personal. Where the Hunger Games tells a story about rebellion and social change as much as it does about its protagonist's efforts to subvert others' use of her, Divergent is interested in a different kind of freedom—from exploitation, yes, but also from the labels society puts on us and the subtle pressures of others' expectations. From our individual fears and from our personal histories. These things may shape us, the Divergent trilogy says, but they do not control us.

Allegiant introduces us to two different, though interrelated, agents of control. First, there's the Bureau of Genetic Welfare, the organization that designed Tris' city hundreds of years ago as an experiment, constantly monitors its goings-on, and steps in (either directly, by wiping memories, or American imperialist–style, by supplying weapons to the side they like best) whenever that experiment's integrity is threatened. Second, there's genetic damage, which—the Bureau claims—controls one's nature so thoroughly that the kindest thing to do for a GD is take away her identity and sequester her in a community where she can be more effectively controlled. (After all, look at the way they live outside those communities, in the fringe!)

At first, *Allegiant*'s focus on the Bureau and genetics makes the book feel like a strange departure from the earlier parts of Tris' story. But it eventually becomes clear that this new world, the one outside the city, is just another version of the one we came to know in *Divergent* and *Insurgent*, that microcosm writ large—a more familiar mirror, a world one step closer to our own, in which the trilogy's earlier themes are reflected. We've seen the unfeeling, arrogant scientists before, in Jeanine and the Erudite, who use their serums and superior knowledge to manipulate and control (in the case of the Dauntless, quite literally). We've seen, in the factions, the idea that there is something innate that determines the course of your life—an inborn quality you can test for, that tells you who you should associate with and what jobs you can do.

In both worlds, Tris proves herself to be a hero. And in both worlds, she does so in a way that shows that heroism is a choice you make, not something you're born with.

In the context of the trilogy's first two books, Tris is our hero because she is Divergent—because she is aware during simulations, but even more important, because she cannot be contained by any one of her city's labels . . . even if she must pretend to be. Her Divergence puts her in danger, but it also means she has a choice: both at the Choosing Ceremony and in every moment after.

The thing is, though, *everyone* in her city has a choice—at least in theory. That's why it's called a *Choosing* Ceremony. Caught between the desire to choose Dauntless and the expectation she will choose Abnegation, Tris defies her upbringing and chooses to be brave. But every one of her fellow sixteen-year-olds has the option to choose as well, not according to social pressure and not according to their test results, but according to their own values—according to who they *want* to be rather than who their family and history has made them. We know Tris' father made his choice this way when he left Erudite for Abnegation. It could be argued Tobias does, too, despite his claim to have chosen Dauntless out of cowardice. Neither of them is Divergent. (Nor are the other transfers in Tris' Dauntless initiate class, for that matter.) And both are successful as transfers. Tobias finishes first in his initiate class; Tris' father is a well-regarded councilman. Their successes are just two of many, many examples in the Divergent trilogy that, even if they are "genetically damaged," human beings have the ability to learn and to grow. Ultimately, *we* are the ones in control of what and who we become.

Other people, whether our parents, our factions, our government, or the tests they design and administer, can try to influence us. They can tell us what they think we should believe, and who they think we should be. They can try to teach and guide us. But what we learn from them—what we do with the information we receive from them about the world and its truths—is up to us. Bureau director David gives Tris her mother's journal, no doubt thinking it will lead Tris to believe in the Bureau's cause. She brings the Bureau down instead. Edith Prior's video was supposed to encourage the city to protect the Divergent and treat them as special, but it only ends up leading Jeanine and her predecessor Norton to kill them.

I'd suggest that, by the end of *Allegiant*, Divergence comes to mean more than just awareness within simulations or having an aptitude for more than one faction. It also suggests awareness, in the real world, of our ability to choose, no matter what our genes say. Of our ability to become, as Tobias says in *Divergent*, "brave, and selfless, *and* smart, *and* kind, *and* honest." Of our ability to think and act independent of influence, whether that influence comes in a serum or from the ones we love.

What does all this contemplation of control and awareness have to do with the book you're holding?

The Divergent trilogy, like any book, is an invitation. It's an invitation to think, and to feel, and to experience. But while a book offers us a story to respond to, it can't control what that response is any more than a video or a "damaged"gene can. Because the way you read a book—the way you react to events and characters, the conclusions you draw—depends on you: your history, your interests, your values.

The Divergent trilogy provides a wealth of ideas for readers to respond to. *Divergent Thinking* collects the responses of more than a dozen of those readers, all of whom also happen to be YA writers themselves. Each came to Tris' story with his or her own influences and experiences, and each came away with—and shares here—something different.

The same faction system led Rosemary Clement-Moore to think about why we enjoy stories that sort us into categories, Jennifer Lynn Barnes to think of a particular way psychologists classify personality, and Julia Karr to think about the inherent dangers a system like the one in the Divergent trilogy presents.

Blythe Woolston came away from the books thinking about fear, while Elizabeth Norris thought about bravery.

Maria V. Snyder and her sixteen-year-old daughter Jenna couldn't read about the Choosing Ceremony without thinking of Jenna's own upcoming choice: of colleges.

The trilogy's setting led Chicago-resident V. Arrow to wonder how the series' landmarks would map onto her city's real ones.

There are plenty more ways to look at the Divergent trilogy than the ones you'll read here—as many as there are people who've read it, I suspect. Still, reading what this particular set of readers saw in the trilogy made my experience of the books significantly richer. It made me a little more aware of what the Divergent trilogy had to offer, and led me to engage both with the story and my own world in new ways.

In fact, you could say that reading these essays made my reading of the trilogy a little more, well, *divergent*.

Leah Wilson
December 2013

You can't talk about the Divergent trilogy without talking about the faction system (and don't worry, we'll be talking about the faction system plenty). The tension between factions—in particular, Erudite and Abnegation—is the chief source of conflict in Divergent, and that tension is only compounded by the introduction, in Insurgent, of the factionless as a united, antifaction force. In Allegiant's biggest reveal, we discover that the philosophies on which the factions were built are integral to the reason Tris' city even exists.

So that's where we start this collection: with Abnegation, Amity, Candor, Dauntless, and Erudite, and with Rosemary Clement-Moore's consideration of our human obsession with sorting ourselves and others, both in history and in literature.

FROM FACTIONS TO FIRE SIGNS

Personality Types
and the Elements of Heroism

ROSEMARY CLEMENT-MOORE

What's your sign?

It's a pickup line so old that dinosaurs used it to hook up down at the Tar Pit Lounge.

Back in the day, in the time between matchmakers and Match.com, people had to go places *in person* when they wanted to meet a potential date. One had to actually start a conversation. Verbally. Face-to-face. It's a feat that the bravest Dauntless might find paralyzing.

Asking someone's astrological sign as a conversational opener would be a great time-saver, relationship-wise, if the date of your birth were any kind of reliable predictor of personality or compatibility. Instead, it really says more about the asker: Ironic hipster? Geriatric pickup artist in a retirement community? Time traveler from the 1970s?

(If you're wondering, I am a Capricorn. According to astrologists, this means I'm industrious, hardworking, ambitious, pragmatic, and tend to be conventional and possibly egotistical. In reality, I am all about "work smarter, not harder," I write fantasy novels, and, at the moment, my hair is dyed blue.)

Even people who *don't* check their horoscope daily sometimes use zodiac signs as a sort of psychological shorthand to describe people—including themselves. Back in college, my BFF (science major, D&D player, fellow Capricorn) explained why two of our social circle couldn't get along: "They're both Leos. It's their way or the highway." (My BFF likes to classify things. Of course she does. She's a scientist, which is a classification in itself.)

As far as our oil-and-water friends were concerned, it was certainly true that each of them liked things the way she liked them. And both *were* born under the Leo sign. Coincidence? Almost definitely.

The difference between being born in a faction or born under a zodiac sign is that while you can't choose your birthdate, you can choose your faction. Or at least you can pick from a limited range of options. Even if you're secretly Divergent, you still have only five choices—six, if you count factionless, which is viewed as a fate worse than death. So, basically, you can be Candor, Amity, Abnegation, Erudite, Dauntless, or screwed.

Dystopian literature is full of worlds where the roles are assigned, rigid, and nonnegotiable. In one of the earliest examples, *Brave New World*, before people are even born they are sorted into Alphas, Betas, Gammas, Deltas, and Epsilons, and assigned jobs like bees in a hive. In Ally Condie's Matched trilogy, teens have everything from their job to their diet to their future spouse picked for them by complicated statistical algorithms. In the Hunger Games trilogy, the twelve (known) districts of Panem are geographical divisions, but their industry and economy affect both the abilities and attitudes of the tributes, so that saying you'd be from District 1 means something radically different than claiming District 12 as your own.

Why do we like books that sort people? When it comes to dystopian series like Divergent, there are multiple answers. One, when you divide people up into factions, districts, ideologies, etc., it's pretty easy to keep them arguing with each other instead of noticing you're taking over the world. Two, as readers, we learn vicariously that the ability to choose for yourself what your role will be, whom you will love, and whom you will (or won't) fight is worth overthrowing the powers that be. And three, stories about enterprising heroes who take down totalitarian regimes make satisfying reading, and often very exciting movies.

But even benign fantasy worlds have their own kind of sorting. J. R. R. Tolkien has Hobbits and Rangers, Elves and Dwarves. And that's just the good guys. J. K. Rowling's world has the four houses of Hogwarts, and Anne McCaffrey's Pern has Holders and Crafters and Dragonriders. World of Warcraft has Horde and Alliance; Dungeons & Dragons has Lawful and Chaotic versions of Good, Evil, and Neutral.

We like to imagine where we would fit into these worlds. We take online quizzes to sort ourselves into Gryffindor or Slytherin or Ravenclaw (does anyone really want to be Hufflepuff?[1]). In conjunction with the *Catching Fire* movie, Fandango.com had a "Which District Are You?" quiz. We choose Horde or Alliance. We create characters that are paladins, thieves, mages, and rogues, and confined to the spells/abilities of their class.

As readers, movie watchers, gamers—let's say, consumers of story media—we enjoy sorting ourselves based on where our sympathies lie, which character captures our emotions, or what type of fantasy world we would want to live in. Even if you wouldn't be a Chaotic Evil Horde Orc in real life, there's a certain charge that comes from declaring yourself the type of person who enjoys playing one.[2]

So what's up with that? An Evil Overlord slapping a label on you is bad, but it's okay to do it to yourself?

Yes and no. Freedom of choice is something worth fighting for. So is knowing who you are, and not being afraid to declare it. But to accomplish our goals, declaring a faction should set our course, not our limits. The Divergent series shows both the power of choice and the cautionary example of being restricted to just one thing.

THE REAL WORLD

Sorting is simply something that we humans like to do. We appreciate having a quick handle by which to grasp

---

[1] I am taking my life in my hands to make this joke. No one who has seen what happens when you poke a badger would cvcr underestimate a Hufflepuff—a perfect example of the dangers of labels and stereotypes.

[2] My aforementioned BFF is one of the most moral people I know, but back in our tabletop-role-playing-game days, she loved playing the evil-genius characters. And she was frighteningly good at it.

the people in our lives. We want to know generally what to expect from someone. For those of us who like to analyze things, we like to, well, analyze people and figure out what makes them do the things they do.

The term *psychiatry* wasn't coined until 1808, but people have been theorizing different ways to sort—and through sorting, better understand—people since there have been people to sort. What we think of as astrology (the zodiac signs, etc.) began back in the B.C. days with the ancient Babylonian astronomers who mapped the seasonal movement of the stars. To their charts the Egyptians, Greeks, and Romans added the idea that personality traits were tied to the stars under which you were born. A guy named Ptolemy wrote it all down in the second century A.D., and Western astrology hasn't changed much since. The Chinese zodiac (year of the Ox, year of the Dragon, etc.) has been around as long or longer. In India, starting about 100 B.C., the Hindu practice of Ayurveda saw mental and physical health as dependent on keeping five different elements in balance.[3] It sorted people into types based on which of those elements predominated. This idea has a parallel in early Western medicine in the form of the four classical "humors"—substances in the body that, when not in balance, would lead to mental and physical illness.[4]

---

[3] This practice is still in use as an alternative medicine.

[4] Pretty much anything that was wrong with you required a surgeon to drain off some of your blood to get rid of the excess bile or phlegm or whatever was making you ill. And even after science had disproven the idea of humors, all the way to the mid-1800s, bloodletting was a common treatment for just about everything from fever to upset stomach, and particularly for psychological problems.

Excesses of these humors were connected to specific personality types. For example, too much black bile made you a melancholy person—very detail and task oriented, but hard to please, with a tendency toward depression. Too much blood made you sanguine—good-natured, passionate, and charismatic, but also impulsive and kind of flighty.

A lot of study has gone into the human psyche since those first ancient astrologers assigned traits to people born under the sign of Capricorn or in the year of the Rabbit. Now we know about genetics and environment and brain chemistry and operant conditioning. But people are still people, and philosophers and scientists remain fascinated by what makes us behave the way we do, in all our variety. (*Why* do they want to know why we do the things we do? Because they're scientists and philosophers, of course. That's what their sort does.)

We don't just sort other people, of course. We also sort ourselves. In our modern world, we start picking factions about the same age Tris picks hers, only we don't call them Dauntless and Erudite and Abnegation. We call them band geeks and nerds and preps and jocks. Or at least, that's what we called them when I was in school. The terminology may have changed, but the sorting has not. The trials of initiation and indoctrination for these groups can be as grueling as anything Tris has to face at Dauntless, and the penalty for failure to fit in can be just as brutal.

Of course, the difference (and it's an important one) is that we don't have to stay factionless. We are allowed to change and evolve and to fall off the train then get up and find a new faction. (Or knit our broken bones and try again to be Dauntless.)

SORTS OF SORTING

Maybe the fact that we're not locked into our choices makes sorting more appealing. Who hasn't taken online personality tests, or sorted themselves (or their friends) into Hogwarts houses? Do *you* know which faction you would choose? Of course you do.

At Hogwarts, I would be a Gryffindor, though that might just be because I know what answers to tick on the online quiz. In *Divergent*'s world I would choose Amity, no question. I'm too much of a wimp to be Dauntless, too selfish to be Abnegation, and too nice to be Candor. I was a science major in college (*What's your major?* is the college version of *What's your sign?*), so I could easily choose Erudite . . . except that they seem like such arrogant jerks. And that's *before* they used the Dauntless as their mind-controlled soldiers.

I know who my Star Wars twin is, which captain of the Enterprise I'm most like, and with which incarnation of Doctor Who I would most enjoy traveling.[5] I also know my friends' answers because they post them on Tumblr. Sorting allows us to declare who we are, and if we're not quite sure yet, turning the lens inward can give us insight into that question.

In real (that is, non-Doctor-Who-related) psychological terms, I am an Introverted Intuitive type, according to Carl Jung. My highest ratings on the Holland Career Code are Creative, Investigation, and Organization. When I take a test based on the Myers-Briggs Type Indicators, I bounce between an INFJ and an INTP, depending on how I'm feeling that day.

The Myers-Briggs Type Indicator is probably the most

---

[5] I was going to say, "It's all in fun!" and then I remembered how serious people get about their favorite Doctor.

popular of these, to the point of being trendy. The MBTI is a matrix of four traits with two options: Extrovert/ Introvert, iNtution/Sensing, Thinking/Feeling, Judging/ Perceiving.[6] Four traits squared means sixteen possible combinations of these type indicators, which gives you sixteen personality types.

The internet has taken the Myers-Briggs types and run with them. You can find self-tests of every variety, and examples of the sixteen personality types as animals, famous people, Star Wars characters, Star *Trek* characters, anime characters, Harry Potter characters . . . This latest pop psychology oversimplification has basically turned the MBTI into the new zodiac.[7]

What you begin to notice, once you've done a lot of this kind of thing, is that the "sorts" have much in common. There aren't many one-to-one correlations, but there is a definite tendency for types to fall into groups that you can map onto each other. It's like human nature can be divided into only so many building blocks, and our psychological variety comes from how you stack them.

IT'S ELEMENTAL

At Tris' Choosing Ceremony are five bowls, each holding an element that represents a faction's core philosophy—Stone (Abnegation), Earth (Amity), Glass (Candor), Coals/Fire

---

[6] If you want to learn more about these traits, a Google search will turn up plenty.

[7] Types are based on personality rather than the unchangeable factor of your birthdate, obviously. Still, this is probably not what Ms. Briggs and Ms. Myers had in mind.

(Dauntless), and Water (Erudite). In a dramatic declaration of intent, each future initiate cuts his or her hand and literally adds his or her blood to their new family.

Natural elements have been used by philosophers as part of sorting systems for ages—the Classical Age, the Renaissance, the New Age . . . The idea is that certain elements have certain properties, which are reflected in certain personality types. Long before the Myers-Briggs personality types were being compared to animals, melancholy people were classified as "Earth" and sanguine daredevils were "Fire."

Different cultures have used different elements, but what's interesting is how much overlap there is between them. The four classical (Western) elements are Earth, Air, Water, and Fire, with a fifth, Aether, sometimes included as the perfect sum of the others. The five Chinese elements (Earth, Water, Fire, Metal, and Wood) may be different, but the personality traits fall into similar clusters. More to the point, the factions in Divergent line up reasonably well, too—especially when compared to Eastern philosophy.

Earth

In Chinese philosophy (as in Western philosophy), earth types are steadfast and dependable. They have a strong sense of duty and they make good administrators. They trust their own senses and they like concrete evidence they can put their hands on. Even though Abnegation uses stone to represent their faction in the Choosing Ceremony and Amity uses earth, Abnegation definitely fits the earth type when it comes to the classical elements—rock steady, dependable, selfless. And stone is, after all, part of the earth.

Earth types can sometimes become stagnant rather than just steady, or dull more than dependable. Taken to the extreme, Abnegation can come off as joyless and colorless—as "stiff" as their nickname implies. On the other hand, the faction's capacity for self-sacrifice for the greater good—like the sacrifices made by many Abnegation leaders, including Tris' parents, to protect the Edith Prior video—shows the strength of this "grounded" element.

Fire

In Chinese astrology, fire types are all about adventure and excitement. Fire is confident, often competitive. (The Western concept of this elemental type emphasizes creativity and innovation, but there's a similar feeling of "action" to this type.)

Dauntless is the obvious faction match here—since they use fire as their elemental symbol, it's sort of a no-brainer. Plus, a form of confidence—courage—is Dauntless' core value. There's also an impulsiveness associated with fire types, and as Tris' interactions with the other initiates make pretty clear, the Dauntless always seem to be spoiling for a fight.

Most of all, Dauntless exhibits the two-sided nature of this element. Fire can keep you alive or it can kill you. Dauntless' initiation and training are physically dangerous, brutal even, with fire's potential to injure or destroy. Like fire, fear must be controlled, but ignoring fear so totally that you no longer exercise reasonable caution can burn you. In other words, the flip side of courage is recklessness. Even the philosophical division within the faction over whether courage means an absence of fear or overcoming it illustrates the dual nature of the fire type.

Metal

Metal is a Chinese elemental sign without a Western equivalent. Those of this type are tenacious and self-reliant, self-confident, and ordered. Metal types have high expectations, which makes me think of Candor's scorn for anyone who doesn't share their determined adherence to the truth. Candor's specialty is the law, which requires both ordered, logical thinking and confidence in one's own judgment. Plus, well, Law and Order. Self-reliance must be a necessity when you're Candor, too, especially since your fellow Candors will not support you if they don't agree with you. "To thine own self be true" can be a lonely philosophy.

But I think the best reason Candor fits here has to do with Candor's Choosing Ceremony element. Candor is represented by glass because they say that honesty is transparent. Metal is opaque, obviously, but both are hard, and both, when their edges are honed, can cut. Candor rejects the idea that absolute honesty can sometimes do more harm than good. They even see tact as a lie. (Glass and metal can also both be reflective. I wonder if the Candor would be such tactless jerks if they had to look honestly at themselves all day?[8])

Wood

Wood types, which also have no Western corollary, are generous, ethical, selfless, and loyal. Their nature is nurturing and peaceful. One traditional symbol of peace is even a piece of wood—an olive branch. Amity uses earth to represent them in the Choosing Ceremony, but their symbol is the tree. They are farmers, and growing things—nurturing them—is their business.

---

[8] I admit some bias here. I had a friend who was totally Candor—talented, funny, wickedly smart, and brutally honest. She truly believed that if someone was hurt by her opinion, it was because they were too sensitive. To be fair, she would have called me an Amity wimp who would rather keep the peace than be completely honest. And she wouldn't have been entirely wrong. So it's all a matter of degrees.

Wood types can become inhibited and passive if they're not careful. Think about it: wood can be so brittle it breaks or so pliant it won't support any weight. Amity shelters Tris, Four, and other faction refugees, but when push comes to shove, they choose to stay impartial rather than help fight Erudite. You could view this as strength of principle regarding their commitment to peace, or you could see it as being weak. The Candor say about the Amity faction that "those who seek peace above all else will always deceive to keep the water calm." Leaving aside the Candor bias, it is true that throughout history people have, in the name of peace, let terrible things happen.[9]

Water

Water is a sign of creativity and intelligence, and water types are philosophers and thinkers. "Deep" thinkers, you might even say. So maybe it's not a coincidence that Erudite picked that symbol to represent their faction in the Choosing Ceremony. To the Erudite, water represents the clarity of knowledge, but water is also changeable, and can be deceptive. Water is (literally) fluid, changing shape depending on its context. And water is not transparent if it's deep enough. Anything could be hiding there in its depths: jellyfish, plankton . . . Jaws.

In both Eastern and Western philosophy, water types are sensitive and emotional. That doesn't sound much like an Erudite principle, but in order to control people (which

---

[9] There's a pretty dead-on real-world example of this in Neville Chamberlain, the British prime minister in the 1930s. In order to preserve peace, he allowed Hitler's Germany to stomp over a good part of Europe until it became clear that Adolph wasn't going to stop unless someone made him.

they definitely know how to do), you have to be sensitive to others' emotions and how to manipulate them.

You may have noticed that each of these elemental types is like the Force: it has a dark side and a light side. The Eastern philosophy of Taoism says (in essence) that everything exists in balance. Each of the five elements has a yin and a yang: dark and light, male and female, productive and destructive.

More than that, each element exists—or should exist—in balance with the others, generating and overcoming. Water nourishes Wood; Wood feeds Fire; Fire creates Earth (ash); Earth yields Metal; Metal enriches Water. Each needs the others to exist. Take out one, and the whole system collapses. Without earth, you cannot grow wood; without metal, you cannot plow the earth to plant crops; without water, you cannot water your plants; and without wood, you can't make a fire and then you'll freeze to death.

The factions work this way on the societal level: each has a role to play to keep Chicago running. Abnegation administrates. Amity produces food. Candor works in law and arbitrates, mediates, and advises the other factions. Dauntless keeps everyone safe and secure and takes on the high-risk jobs. Erudite are the doctors and scientists that improve life for everyone.

But internally, the factions aren't balanced at all; they prize one quality at the expense of all others. And an unbalanced system is an unhealthy one, allowing corruption (*ahem*Jeanine*ahem*) to set in.

Any quality, no matter how admirable, becomes a negative when taken to the extreme.

Courage becomes recklessness.

Pushing someone to their limits becomes bullying.

Honesty becomes rudeness and self-absorption (i.e., my truth is more important than your feelings).

Peace becomes passivity (or passive-aggressiveness).

Self-sacrificing austerity becomes martyrdom and/or a joyless existence.

Erudition becomes valuing knowledge over people.

FATAL FICTIONAL FLAWS

In fiction, a character's imbalance of temperament often shows up as a fatal or tragic flaw. In Shakespeare's *Romeo and Juliet*, Romeo is definitely a Dauntless, judging by his quick-fire changes of affection, his slaying of Juliet's cousin Tybalt without thinking about her reaction, his taking poison without wondering why Juliet's body is still warm after two days in a tomb. He fears nothing, even when he should, and he dies pretty much of an excess of emotional impetuosity.

For an example of a tragic flaw that doesn't end in death and disaster, there's Prospero, from another Shakespeare play, *The Tempest*. Even banished to a deserted island, he is an obvious Erudite, arrogant about his books and spells and how learned and artistic he is. If he had been paying more attention to running his country and less to his studies, his brother wouldn't have been able to steal his kingdom, and Prospero wouldn't have ended up stranded on that island in the first place (and then there would be no play).

Then there's Batman. He's not so bad off as Romeo or Prospero, but he's not the poster child for self-actualized balance, either. Batman is, in a word, broody. He is melancholic like earth types, weighed down by his sense of duty and the obligation of vengeance. Abnegation seems like an odd faction for a billionaire playboy, but Batman . . . he's got a tendency toward martyrdom. Bruce Wayne may have a luxurious manor, but that's just for show. The bat has a *cave*. If that's not self-denial, I don't know what is.

Contrast that with Superman, who has a much more balanced temperament. He's got the sense of justice and duty of the Abnegation, the honesty of a Candor, the courage of the Dauntless (I'm sure it helps to be invulnerable to almost everything), the brains of the Erudite (with a little alien technology to help), and even though he's action oriented, he's got Amity's love of peace. Superman doesn't pick fights, though he certainly will finish them.

Of course, Superman can be all the factions in one. He's, you know, Superman. He's the ultimate Divergent.

REAL HEROES ARE DIVERGENT

Let's now swing back around to our earlier question: "Why do we like books that sort people?" The answer comes down, I think, to a paradox:

1. Humans like to sort things.
2. Humans like heroes who defy sorting.

Basically, we like books that put our heroes into boxes so that we can enjoy watching them break out.

I am a complete sucker for the girl-has-to-dress-as-a-boy trope. It doesn't matter if she's saving the family farm or avenging her father or rescuing the family's honor. Disney's *Mulan* is a ready example of this. We even get a song early in the movie about how Mulan doesn't fit the mold of the perfect Chinese daughter. She takes her aged father's place when one male from each family is drafted into the army, so you know she's self-sacrificing (Abnegation) and brave (Dauntless). When she gets to training, she's outclassed—like Tris, she's had the wrong sort of training for the situation and has to catch up with her peers—so she has to work smarter, not harder (Erudite). Mulan is Divergent.

A less action-oriented example of an expectations-defying character is Jo March. Almost the first thing we learn about her is that she's a tomboy and likes to defy convention. She's the boldest of the four girls in *Little Women*, so definitely Dauntless. But she's also a reader and a writer, and she's *very* proud of the fact—so she's got some Erudite tendencies, too. Over the course of the story, she shows examples of all five factions, as she learns about forgiveness, selflessness, peaceful acceptance, and writing a book that is true and honest to her heart. Jo March is Divergent.

Enough literature. Let's talk about The Avengers. Because not every hero can be *everything* all on their own. Sometimes heroes need buddies to round them out.

The Avengers are a heroic team. Their group works because it's balanced; it includes examples of all five factions in individuals. Tony Stark: Erudite, because *obviously*. Captain America: Candor, because of truth, justice, and the American way. Thor: Amity, because he keeps trying to make peace with Loki and Loki keeps taking advantage of him. (Also, Amity's symbol at the Choosing Ceremony is Earth, and Thor is a little thick.) The Hulk: Dauntless, because he is all emotion and impulse. (Also, HULK SMASH!) Agent Coulson: Abnegation, of course. He's the administrative arm of S.H.I.E.L.D., a behind-the-scenes sort of fellow, but most of all, he sacrifices himself for the team.

Constructing a balanced team isn't an exact science. The other team members—Black Widow, Hawkeye, and Nick Fury—also go into making the Avengers function. It's not as simple as "equal parts Amity, Dauntless, etc." (And you might have a different opinion for which Avenger should represent which faction.) But thanks to the individual talents and strengths of its members, the team as a whole is Divergent.

Being a part of a balanced team can make the individuals more balanced, too. Over the course of the movie, I think most of the Avengers have to become a little more Divergent. (One of the reasons I like that movie so much is that each character has their own Growth Moment.) Being superheroes, they're all a bit Dauntless. Bruce Banner has to make peace with his anger so he can control becoming the Hulk. Black Widow is a very different type of Erudite than Tony Stark, being both canny and shifty, but she also has a moment of real self-honesty when she talks about the "red in her ledger."

The biggest change, however, comes to Tony Stark, who is arguably (as in, I will make this argument with anyone) the film's main hero in two ways: 1) even though saving the world takes the whole team, it's Stark that does That Thing At The End, and 2) in order to do it, he is the character who makes the biggest transformation.

He starts out a textbook Erudite—too smart for his own good, and smart aleck to go with it. Billionaire genius playboy. He even lives in a tower full of gadgets and tech like the Erudite in Chicago. Throughout the movie, the other Avengers challenge him about his lack of honesty, empathy, and selflessness, and he deflects them with wisecracks. But in the pivotal big bad boss fight, it isn't being smarter than everyone else that allows him to save the world. It's being brave and selfless. Iron Man doesn't start out the film as Divergent, but he ends it that way.

In *Divergent*, I don't think it's an accident that Tris' friends and allies at Dauntless are faction transfers—besides the fact that the newbies would stick together. They are a divergent group: Christina is from Candor, Will from Erudite, Tobias/Four from Abnegation. (Amity is under-represented, but as I said before, it's not an exact science.)

Tris is identified as Divergent by the aptitude test very early on, but she has to keep it a secret. Obviously, it influences her at the Choosing Ceremony, and she waffles between factions—and symbolically, between the facets of her personality. But she doesn't really *own* it until the end of the first book. Still, even before that, it's when she shows her Divergence that Tris has her most heroic moments. Taking Al's place in front of the target was an act of bravery, but also of empathy and self-sacrifice. Tris is clever enough to work out what Erudite is really doing with the serums they inject into the Dauntless, and later, to create a plan for getting back into Dauntless headquarters to stop the simulation. She's also brave enough to enact that plan, but in the process she must also lead Caleb, her father, and Marcus, talking them through the hard parts of jumping from a moving train (onto a roof, no less). That takes empathy, an Abnegation trait, as well as leadership.

Not that Tris is perfectly Divergent. There's not much of Amity in her. She is not big on peace or forgiveness. Honesty isn't her strongest virtue, either. And while she is very smart, Tris acknowledges the Abnegation part of herself more than she does the Erudite.

However, in the climactic confrontation with the

simulation-controlled Tobias, it really is all three of her Divergent aspects that allow her to save him, and herself: cleverness to come up with an action drastic enough to reach him, self-sacrifice to put the gun into his hand, and a hell of a lot of bravery to trust her plan would work.

DIVERGENCE IN ACTION

In *Allegiant*, the whole faction rug gets ripped out from under us. Instead of factions, our heroes are struggling with questions of individual identity. But never has being Divergent been more important. Not because of genetic purity or superperson status, but because the old paradigm has been erased, and being just one thing is no longer an option. Decisions and alliances are no longer confined to what a faction demands. That can be overwhelming if you're used to a limited number of choices.

But the Divergent have always—at least privately—had more choices, because their Divergence allows them to adapt. A Divergent hero can weigh her options. She can use brains or brawn, be honest or be crafty, compromise for peace or stick to her guns.

After the revelations in *Allegiant*, it's worth pointing out that Divergence is not merely a genetic factor. Tris might be Divergent in biology, but Tobias is Divergent in action. The five faction symbols tattooed on his back show he understands the need for balance between the factions and their guiding principles. All through the series he doesn't just evidence bravery or selflessness. He demonstrates intelligence and kindness. He learns honesty and peace.

Divergence, whether it's in your genes, your upbringing, or the process of learning, is what allows you to make individual choices. It allows for bravery, honesty, reconciliation, wisdom, and sacrifice whenever each, or all, are necessary.

Over our lifetimes, we choose factions over and over again. We leave one behind and choose another. We have the freedom of concentric or overlapping circles of friends and family. We don't have to pick one path, one trait, one ideal, and close our minds to all others. We can be Divergent. And we definitely should.

Rosemary Clement-Moore *is the author of a bunch of awesome books like* The Splendor Falls, Texas Gothic, *and* Spirit and Dust, *which have been recommended by the ALA Best Books for Teens, the TAYSHAS reading list, and her mother's book club. She's a water sign, an introvert, her patronus is an otter, and New!Kirk is her Enterprise Captain. Besides internet quizzes, she is addicted to coffee, books, knitting, and the Discovery Channel. She lives in Fort Worth, Texas, with a miniature yeti disguised as a Pomeranian.*

There are a lot of ways to sort people, and as we saw in Rosemary's essay, these methods often have a lot in common, even going back thousands of years. Jennifer Lynn Barnes, YA novelist and PhD in psychology, maps the Divergent trilogy's factions onto another real-life method for describing our personalities, this one favored by modern psychologists: the Five Factor Model, otherwise known as the Big Five.

DIVERGENT PSYCHOLOGY

Jennifer Lynn Barnes

Veronica Roth has stated that she got the idea for *Divergent* while studying exposure therapy in Psych 101, but the psychology underlying the world of *Divergent* and threaded throughout the series goes far beyond studies on what it means to confront and overcome our fears. Psychology can explain the significance of the five factions, what it really means to be Divergent, and why, as readers, we're faced with the same challenges that Tris confronts: to look beyond the simulation, to carve out an identity, to find the place where we belong.

In our case, the *simulation* is the book itself. When I'm not writing young adult novels, I study the science of fiction and the question of why we get so invested in fictional stories. Why, psychologists ask, do we invest so much time and spend so much money on things that we know are not real? And why is it that *knowing* that Tris and Four aren't real doesn't render her death painless for us as readers? Why would we ever cry real tears for people we know are make-believe?

One answer that scientists have come up with to this question is that fictional stories are simulations—and, yes, they do use that exact word. Even though we *know* these fictional stories are not real, we *feel* like they are. As Tris comments inside her fear landscape, "Simulations aren't real; they pose no real threat to me, so logically, I shouldn't be afraid of them." And yet, despite knowing that the simulation isn't real, Tris' reactions to it are, as she puts it, "visceral" (*Divergent*). So, too, are our reactions as readers.

My goal for this essay is to dig beneath the surface of the simulation, with an eye to what the psychological sciences can tell us about the books. Like Tris, we can't just turn off our emotions in response to something that *seems* so real, but we *can* use our awareness of the simulation to ask why the world Veronica Roth has built is so compelling. The answer, I am going to argue, is that the faction system challenges us as readers to ask the same questions that plague Tris throughout the series:

Who are we? What are we? And where do we belong?

THE FACTIONS, PERSONALITY, AND THE BIG FIVE

The faction system is introduced to us as a way in which groups of people dedicate themselves to different virtues. Each faction, we are told in *Divergent*, was founded on the belief that a specific vice was to blame for the world's evils. Those who blamed dishonesty formed Candor; those who blamed cowardice became the Dauntless; those who eschewed selfishness became Abnegation; those who despised ignorance became Erudite; and those who swore off aggression became Amity. In this sense, the Choosing Ceremony asks teenagers to decide which virtue they want to live their lives by. It is up to them, Tris and her age-mates are told by a somber Marcus, "to decide what kind of people they will be" (*Divergent*).

On the surface, then, the ceremony asks young people to decide what they believe. What they *value*. Choosing to switch factions reflects a rejection of everything a person has been raised to believe, parallel in some ways to a child who has been raised in one religious tradition choosing to convert to another. And yet, for all that the factions are purportedly based on virtues, I do not think the powerful and compelling concept the faction system taps into really *is* belief.

Tris seems to come to a similar conclusion herself. In *Divergent*, when Four asks Tris if she thinks she made the right choice in coming to Dauntless, she says that she doesn't think there *was* a choice. For Tris, the ceremony isn't about deciding who she *will be*. It is about acknowledging who she *already is*. "I didn't jump off the roof because I wanted to be like the Dauntless," Tris realizes midway through *Divergent*. "I jumped off because I already was like them, and I wanted to show myself to them."

At their core, these five factions are not merely about what a person believes or what they value. To my psychologist's eye, what the faction system is really tapping into is the enduring internal traits that make us who we are: our *personalities*. This is occasionally acknowledged in the text: the vices that the factions are fighting against are initially referred to as faults in "human personality." In *Insurgent*, Jeanine describes Divergents as having "flexible personalities," while Fernando refers to transferring from Abnegation to Dauntless as "a leap in personality." Even those who have been raised within the faction system seem to recognize that choosing a faction has as much to do with your aptitude for specific traits as your belief about which virtue is the most virtuous of them all.

What the residents of Tris' community don't seem to realize, however, is just how closely their faction system maps onto personality psychology more broadly. Just as there are five factions, psychologists refer to the "Big Five" personality traits: five traits that can describe the vast variation we see in human personality—each corresponding to one of the five factions in the Divergent series. Some of the parallels are obvious—you don't need to be a psychologist to realize that Amity has a lot of parallels with the trait referred to as *Agreeableness*—while others require parsing your way through the text with an eye for detail.

Dauntless: Openness to Experience

The first of the Big Five is a trait referred to as *Openness to Experience*. People who are low in openness are frequently described as being cautious, clinging to routines, and disliking the idea of going outside of their comfort zones. On the opposite end of the spectrum, we have people high in openness, who tend to be curious. They *like* hearing new ideas and doing things that they've never done before. They are not cautious, but instead—as the term suggests—are open to whatever new experiences the world has to offer. Openness to experience tends to co-occur with a variety of other things, among them creativity, risk taking, and sensation seeking.

My college roommate, when she takes personality tests,

scores off the charts on the openness variable—and I cannot help but notice that this is the same college roommate who has decided that we will be spending her bachelorette party skydiving. The college roommate who once talked me into zip-lining. The college roommate who read *Divergent* and told me, with all confidence, that she would be Dauntless.

The parallels between Dauntless and this dimension of personality go beyond the fact that the Dauntless are a skydiving, zip-lining, jumping-off-buildings kind of group. Openness isn't just about being open to physical risks. Just as there are three levels to the Dauntless initiation—the physical, the emotional, and the mental—openness to experience also operates on all three levels. Tris is high in openness not only because she's willing to jump off a moving train, but also because she's the type of person who is curious about what's outside the fence—and willing to go off into the unknown to get her answer. Toward the beginning of *Divergent*, Tori actually comments on Tris' curiosity, saying that she's "never met a curious Abnegation before." (Tris and the others may assume that curiosity is the reason she shows an aptitude for Erudite, but I would argue that this trait, as much as a desire to be fearless, is what makes Tris choose Dauntless—and that Tris' Erudite side taps into a different quality altogether, one that we'll return to later.)

Interestingly, people who are high in openness to experience also tend to be more easily hypnotized than other individuals—which seems fitting, given that the Dauntless end up more or less neurologically hypnotized into doing Jeanine's bidding at the end of the first book. Equally striking is the fact that the openness variable tends to decline with age—and the Dauntless in the Divergent series force older faction members out.

Abnegation: Extraversion (and the Lack Thereof)

In many ways, Abnegation is the faction that it is hardest to classify in terms of the Big Five—until you realize that this faction does not just require putting other people first; they endorse a full-scale denial of the self. As part of Abnegation, Tris is only allowed to look in a mirror once every three months. She and her family do not celebrate their birthdays. The Abnegation are told they must try to forget themselves and fade into the background. When the Abnegation flirt, they flirt "in the tentative way known only to the Abnegation" (*Divergent*), exchanging shy looks and slight smiles. Tris says that it is difficult for the Abnegation to make friends because "it's impossible to have real friendship when no one feels like they can accept help or even talk about themselves" (*Divergent*).

From this perspective, I would argue that the Big Five personality trait that Abnegation maps onto is actually *Extraversion*—or more specifically, introversion, the word we use to describe people who are extremely low on the extraversion personality scale. The extraverted individual is talkative, assertive, and the life of the party—not someone that anyone else would ever refer to as a *Stiff*. Extraverts *like* being the center of attention. Introverts, in contrast, tend to be described as solitary and reserved. Introverted individuals keep in the background, they don't like to draw attention to themselves, and they can be hard to get to know.

When Tris expresses a desire in *Divergent* to be "loud and daring and free," she is expressing a desire to shake off her introverted roots and become more extraverted. She transfers to Dauntless not only because she is curious and longs to experience a wider range of what life has to offer, but also because she is tired of feeling like she has to keep everything inside. She is tired of fading into the background, tired of wearing gray clothes and behaving in an unassuming way, tired of trying to forget herself, and tired of being forgotten.

In some ways, this aspect of Tris' story parallels the classic teen movie trope of an introverted teenager making the conscious decision to break out of her shell. Shortly after Tris joins Dauntless, Christina even gives her a makeover, replacing her gray clothes with a little black dress, lining her eyes with eyeliner, and declaring, "I'm going for noticeable" (*Divergent*). And yet, even after Tris transfers to Dauntless, aspects of her Abnegation roots remain. She is never a *look at me, look at me* kind of brave. She leads quietly and by example. For many people—even Four—she remains difficult to know.

Erudite: Conscientlousness

The third faction that Tris shows an aptitude for is Erudite, the faction that prizes knowledge and intelligence above all else. And yet, the Erudite are not defined merely by being smart. After all, there are plenty of intelligent people in the other factions, too. Rather, the Erudite seem to be a very specific kind of smart—extremely organized, unemotional, almost pathological in their devotion to logic and reason.

In terms of the Big Five, this cluster of traits maps onto *Conscientiousness*. Conscientiousness is associated with self-discipline: perfectionists, workaholics, and those driven to achieve all rate high on this trait. Conscientious individuals plan ahead. They pay attention to details. They are highly organized, highly efficient, and they finish what they start.

Sound like anyone we know?

The Erudite are known as meticulous record keep-ers. Jeanine is slavishly devoted to her master plan. She's a "walking, talking computer" (*Divergent*). Caleb finds Jeanine persuasive at least in part because he, too, has a thirst not just for knowledge, but for singularity of purpose. Even Cara, in the final book in the trilogy, founds the Al-legiant to work toward a two-pronged goal: to overthrow Evelyn and to send a scouting party outside of the city. The way she presents this to the others feels almost like she's checking items off a to-do list, even if those items involve "escape to unknown" and "rebel." When she ultimately discovers that the plan has no meaning—that the faction system is part of an experiment and the Edith Prior tape was contrived—she is lost. Cara doesn't know who she is without the plan, without purpose: "I'm an Erudite, you know," she tells Tris. "It's the only thing I am" (*Allegiant*).

Tris has an aptitude for Erudite not because she's stu-dious or a lover of books, but because she is a strategist. Whether it's for capture the flag or a preemptive strike against those playing with the lives of those she loves, she is a planner who will go to great lengths to see things through to the end. Ultimately, the difference between Tris and Jeanine is not in their ability to form plans or to ex-ecute them—it's the fact that Jeanine is willing to do so at great costs to *others*, and Tris does so no matter the cost to *herself*.

Candor: Low on Neuroticism

Candor prizes honesty. It is difficult at first to see how this could correspond to any of the five traits we use to clas-sify human personalities—until we unpack a bit more about what this means on a day-to-day basis. The Candor wear black and white; they don't get bogged down in shades of gray. Their manifesto proudly declares, "We have no suspicions and no one suspects us" (*Divergent* bonus materials). Candor initiation involves the forced confession of an initiate's darkest secrets. Afterward, no one has anything to hide, and as a result, they do not have to worry about the consequences of telling the truth.

The personality trait associated with worrying about how other people view you is *Neuroticism*. People who are high in neuroticism are prone to embarrassment. They tend to be insecure and highly anxious. Other people might describe them as *sensitive*. In other words, they are the exact personality type that could not survive in Candor. In contrast, individuals who are low in neuroticism are not easily embarrassed. They are confident, tend not to worry, and are not easily bothered. Both aspects of Candor—always telling the truth yourself and weathering the emotional costs of constantly being told what other people think of you—require a personality type that is relatively immune to anxiety. For individuals high in neuroticism, things are not always black and white—and the difference between gray and dark gray might be worth agonizing over in and of itself.

During her simulation, Tris proves that she does not have an aptitude for Candor by lying when asked if she knows a man. In that moment, her heart pounds. She is overcome with anxiety and convinced—*convinced*—that if she tells the truth, something awful will happen. That fear—of an unknown, ambiguous *something*—is a prime example of neuroticism, and ultimately, it's the reason that Tris adamantly does *not* belong in Candor.

Amity: Agreeableness

Finally, we have Amity, the faction that most clearly maps onto one of the Big Five—so much so that it might as well be called *agreeableness*. Individuals who are high on agreeableness are friendly, warm, and cooperative. They may be overly trusting. They tend to lose arguments—and may refuse to argue altogether. Highly agreeable individuals avoid conflict, find it difficult to hold grudges, and may express little to no desire for vengeance when they are wronged.

When I take personality tests, this tends to be the variable on which I score the highest. With the possible exception of a life-or-death struggle, I cannot imagine hitting another person—and yelling is almost as out of the question. I do stand up for what I believe in, but I also pick my battles, and they tend to be very *polite* battles. Once, when I was crossing the street and got nicked by a car, I apologized to the person who hit me.

In *Insurgent*, when Marcus refuses to share the secret of Edith Prior's video with Johanna, she makes a similar apology. Rather than confronting him for being secretive, she apologizes for whatever it is that *she's* done to make *him* think she's not trustworthy. When the Amity vote, it is expected that it will be unanimous; and when they vote to allow Tris and company to stay at the Amity compound in the beginning of *Insurgent*, the condition on that invitation is that the guests aren't allowed to even *reference* the conflict.

As indicated by her original test results, Tris is fairly low on agreeableness. She describes herself as "not nice," and while she is extremely loyal and loves fiercely, she also gets a rush out of physical confrontations and violence. And yet, if Tris *were* higher on agreeableness, she likely wouldn't be able to rebel the way she does. In order to fight for what one believes in, a person *has* to be able to fight.

WHAT IS DIVERGENCE?

I believe that part of the appeal of the Divergent series comes from the fact that in presenting readers with these five factions, Roth has essentially offered up a personality test that asks readers to answer the same question that Tris must: Who are *you*? Where do *you* belong?

Are you high on agreeableness? Maybe you belong in Amity. Score off the charts in openness to experience, and you might be a better fit for Dauntless. The caveat to this exercise, however, is that unlike the factions in *Divergent*, the Big Five personality traits don't compete with each other. They were identified as traits of interest *because* each one seems to exist independent of the others. A person can be open *and* agreeable *and* neurotic *and* conscientious *and* extraverted—or any combination thereof. You might score high on all five traits—or two of the five, or three, or none. Being highly agreeable doesn't mean you can't also be open to new experiences, any more than being introverted means that you can't be conscientious.

For this reason, it is likely that many—if not most—of the people who read this series are themselves Divergent. I'd probably be Amity or Erudite, but I'd bet my simulation wouldn't rule out Abnegation.

In *Allegiant*, we learn that most of the individuals in Tris' community have a genetic modification that causes them to score at an unnatural extreme on one trait. The scientists in the book describe the original modification as an attempt at getting rid of negative traits, but for traits that exist along a spectrum, no matter which way you frame it, the end result is one and the same: eliminating aggression *is* increasing agreeableness. Either way, "genetically damaged" individuals end up with unusually extreme scores in one and only one trait—be they extremely high (fearless and open) or extremely low (selfless and not extraverted in the least), while the genetically "healed" individuals—the Divergents—score more like the rest of us. In this way, the series itself confirms the idea that in its natural state, human personality is not typically driven by one extreme trait that drowns out the rest.

This explains a great deal about why so many people in Tris' world seem to have no problem dedicating themselves to a single faction; however, there is a large part of me that believes that the scientists in *Allegiant* got it wrong—that Divergence, as depicted throughout the series, is not simply a matter of being "genetically pure." Throughout the first two books, Divergence is defined by two things: an affinity for more than one faction and the ability to stay aware in the simulations. The scientists consider the latter to be nothing more than a "genetic marker," a convenient sign that someone has reached a certain milestone of genetic purity.

I don't believe them.

These are the same scientists who believe that war did not exist before genetic modification. They've lost touch with history; I believe they have also lost touch with some pretty major tenets of science, including what it means to *do* science in the first place. The scientific method prioritizes asking questions in a way that *could* disprove your theory. If there is no outcome that would change your conclusion— say, that "genetic damage" is associated with violence and can be healed through the world's oddest selective breeding experiment—then what you are doing *is not science*.

If you have been raised from childhood to view your theory as fact, even as you are being taught how to conduct your "experiment," what you are doing *is not science*.

If you twist your data to fit your theory by ignoring any data points that could call your theory into question—like Marcus, a "genetically pure" man who is nonetheless violent—what you are doing *is not science*.

And if you are a geneticist who—for reasons that escape me—believes that the way to get rid of a mutation is to take tons of people who have that mutation and *breed them together*, I reserve the right to side-eye your scientific credentials.

All of which goes to say that there are plenty of reasons *not* to take Matthew and company at their word about what it means to be Divergent. I tend to think that the fact that Divergents are aware during simulations isn't just some genetic marker; to me, it is the single biggest clue about what being Divergent might—at least symbolically—mean.

I believe that being Divergent means being *aware*—not just aware that the simulations aren't real, but *self-aware*. We all vary in the degree to which we demonstrate each of the Big Five personality traits; to me, what makes Tris special is not so much the fact that she scores at the extremes on three of the five, but the fact that she is keenly *aware* of where she stands. She is constantly analyzing herself, breaking her personality down into parts, actively attempting to construct an identity, and aware of all of the ways in which the various identities she tries on do not fit. She is critical of people who lack this kind of self-awareness: she judges Caleb not only for being "despicable," but also for having "no understanding of how despicable he is" (*Allegiant*).

When we get to see Four's perspective on Tris, he notes that while what Cara has gone through has made her certain of herself, Tris' suffering has just made her cling to her uncertainties *more*. Tris knows what she doesn't know, and she is able to use that level of awareness to come to a striking conclusion about human nature: "That internal war doesn't seem like a product of genetic damage—it seems completely, purely *human*" (*Allegiant*).

Ultimately, it is Tris' insight into her own vices and virtues, her own wants and needs, that sets her apart. She recognizes how very much she is driven by the need to belong. She sees the parallels between the factions inside the fence and the divisions outside the fence. And ultimately, she realizes that words and labels may not fulfill the human need to belong as fully as relationships do. When she dies, it is not as a "GP" or a "Divergent," not as "Abnegation" or "Dauntless," but as a sister and a lover, a daughter and a friend.

I like to think that Tris' death serves a purpose, not just in the atrocities it prevents, but also in the way that it might cause other people to introspect, to question who they are, their vices, their virtues. I like to think that for the second time in her life, Tris has seen a group of people dazed and sleepwalking, and she's woken them up.

I like to imagine that in the wake of losing Tris, Caleb and Four—and so many others—are a little more Divergent now. ·

Jennifer Lynn Barnes *has degrees in psychology, psychiatry, and cognitive science. She's the author of twelve books for young adults, including the* Raised By Wolves *series,* Every Other Day, *and* The Naturals. *When she's not writing about teens confronting extraordinary circumstances, she studies the psychology of fiction and why we like it.*

Let's pretend, for a few thousand words, that Divergent's world is not an invention, but a reality—one that evolved from (or, more accurately, given the Bureau's involvement, was constructed from) our own. Could we locate the landmarks of Divergent's future Chicago on a map of today's, using what we know of both the real city and the clues provided by Tris in the text? In her essay, V. Arrow has done exactly that.

MAPPING DIVERGENT'S CHICAGO

V. Arrow

I know all the words she's saying—except I'm not sure what [a] "united states" is—but they don't make sense to me all together . . . Chicago. It's so strange to have a name for the place that was always just home to me. It makes the city smaller in my mind.

—*Allegiant*

Before Tris Prior and the rest of her small group come together to escape from their city near the beginning of *Allegiant*, all she knows is Chicago—but not Chicago, Illinois. Not Chicago, in Cook County, in the United States of America. In the years between now and the time *Divergent* takes place, the Chicago we know has become a bubble-nation on the former shore of Lake Michigan.

To Tris, because the city is everything, it isn't a city at all, but an entity—a world—unto itself, with its own set of rules, regulations, landmarks, and history. Although the names remain for places like Navy Pier, the Merchandise Mart, even Randolph and State Streets and Michigan Avenue, there are no reference points for Tris to know what they were built upon. The names, and roots, of landmarks in Chicago's long history have been lost, just as much as the genetic codes the Bureau hopes the Divergent can heal. What would determine which names would stay and take on new meanings and which would fade away and take on new titles, like the Hub? (*Millennium* means nothing if you don't know the year. What does *Monroe* mean to a city that's never known US presidents?)

While Chicago's rich history may be unknown to Tris, it does seem to continue on through many of the characteristics of the factions. In fact, when David explains to Tris and her fellow refugees early on in their stay at O'Hare Airport that Chicago has been the most successful experiment, enough to have become a model for other experimental cities, it brings to mind one of the Windy City's other long-standing nicknames—*The City That Works*. "Your city is one of those experiments for genetic healing, and by far the most successful one, because of the behavioral modification portion. The factions, that is" (*Allegiant*).

When I first began to map the Divergent trilogy's Chicago, the foremost question in my mind was, *How can an entire dystopian world scale down to one city?* Does each faction have its own fenced-off territory, like the districts of Panem or the provinces of *Matched*, or can a Dauntless member—theoretically—take a stroll down the street that Candor's headquarters is on? Is Chicago still a functioning *city* at all?

The placements of the faction headquarters in relation to the Hub and the train line would have to answer that question, since Tris spends most of the peacetime of the series in initiation, unable to leave the Dauntless compound, and then is on the run during the battle after Jeanine's attack simulation. While Tris is the only window to the Divergent trilogy's Chicago that we have, her Chicago—her world—is a place divided by war, not just by factions.

Today's Chicago, too, is a segmented city, but it doesn't have separate addresses for its identities the way New York City does. Being in The Loop or Devon Avenue in Chicago does not impart the same feeling as being in Chinatown or Greektown or Wrigleyville, not to mention the vast and spidering network of suburbs that make up "Chicagoland." The identity of Chicago is, and has always been, one of rivalries: Cubs versus Sox, North Side versus South Side, Gino's East versus Giordano's deep-dish pizza. The darker underbelly of these rivalries, of course, are the divisive issues of race and economics that have been a part of Chicago since its inception: some historians believe that the modern concept of the street gang began in Chicago, and Chicago's history of organized crime is notorious. Government cor ruption and police brutality plague the city's history. Communities are, for their own protection, often insular, despite the lack of strict geographic boundaries.

In other words, for what Divergent's world must be, Chicago is the perfect setting.

Like Veronica Roth, I'm from Chicagoland, that network of commuter suburbs surrounding the city, so I had some idea of the geography the story deals with, and some preconceptions from my casual initial reads of the series: I thought Amity might exist in Lake Forest, a suburb just outside the city on the shore of Lake Michigan; Candor would fit well with a headquarters at the Dirksen Courthouse on Dearborn, where the famed mafia trials "Operation Family Secrets" took place in the 1970s. Abnegation seemed to me to fit Andersonville, an area of the city that is quaint and less overtly urban, with deep Swedish and German Lutheran roots. Because Chicago is a city with so much culture and such deep intellectual roots, there were a myriad of places that I thought Erudite might fit—the current-day campus of the University of Chicago; the Museum Campus, home to the Field Museum, Adler Planetarium, and the Shedd Aquarium; maybe the Museum of Science and Industry; or even Northwestern University, also in a suburb off the lake. A closer reading was definitely needed.

And of course, I had to figure out the location of the Dauntless headquarters. For them, I had no idea.

An idea integral to envisioning a map of Divergent's Chicago is that, despite the factions and their alleged rigidity, faction members were, except during their initiation phases, allowed to travel more or less freely through the city: Tris, Uriah, and other Dauntless travel from Dauntless headquarters to go zip-lining, Tris is able to visit Caleb at the Erudite compound, and all five factions attend the same school until they are sixteen. Such a large range of movement is characteristic of Chicago and sets it apart from many other cities even today: while most native New Yorkers, for example, live their entire lives within ten square blocks, Chicago and its citizens are hugely motile, with most workers within the city commuting from outer suburbs every day by car, train, bus, and sometimes, within the city, water taxis. One thing that Tris' Chicago certainly inherited from our own is a sense of movement and a need for working transportation lines: in *Insurgent*, we learn that even the factionless depend on the trains. This reliance on and ability to freely use transit sets Divergent apart from other popular dystopian series, where people live in small radii, and traveling into, or even near, the bases of other disenfranchised groups is tantamount to treason.

The only place we see any kind of "turf" rigidity in the Divergent series is in the barring of Abnegation from Erudite land in the first book—their mutual disdain precludes them from allowing anyone wearing the other faction's colors to pass through unnoticed and unscathed. And given Chicago's deep history with gangs—one of the most notorious aspects of the city, and one that plagues its citizenry every day in tragic, tangible consequences—their movements and rivalries seemed like a useful model for understanding how the different factions might be mapped out.

As of 2012, over 400 gangs were active in Chicago proper, with more operating within the soft limits of "Chicagoland." It would be almost impossible to create a social system like the factions and base it in Chicago without drawing comparisons to gang culture: the idea of "faction before blood"; the restrictions of colors, tattoos, and even hairstyles and naming conventions available to each faction, used not only to mark brethren, but to differentiate them from outsiders; and of course, the catastrophic violence when members of these alliances clash.

When we think about the Divergent trilogy as fiction, we might guess that Roth's upbringing in Chicago's suburbs, and the clouding proximity of gang culture in the area, may have influenced her in creating Divergent's factions (even if indirectly). Similarly, if we think of the trilogy and Tris' city as real, we might guess that being located in what was originally Chicago, with its strong gang presence, may have influenced its development—in particular, the idea that factions might be a useful way of controlling its people's behavior at all. At the Bureau of Genetic Welfare, David tells Tris that Chicago was the first city to have factions—a way to modulate and enforce standards of behavior. The factions certainly seem to function according to research on gang member psychology:

"Sociologists believe that a gang will take on the morals, or lack of morals, of the worst members . . . this behavior can be explained as 'group dynamics,'" writes Lou Savelli of *Police Magazine*.[1] This seems to mirror the extent of Jeanine's hold over the Erudite, particularly over the low-level informant and new recruit Caleb, and the way that she and the Dauntless leaders, such as Eric, build their own codes of ethics into the workings of the factions under their control. Tobias, in *Divergent*, noted that with Eric—a ruthless bully—as one of the leaders of the Dauntless, the Dauntless as a whole had become meaner, more lawless, and more violent.

While the Bureau may have seen the factions as a way to encourage docile behavior through nurture, eventually the behavior modification became less an act of nurture within the factions and more of a way to define the factions' inherent, and enacted, differences: Tris becomes accustomed to jumping from trains, to getting tattoos, to eating Dauntless food and thinking "selfishly." Likewise, she notices changes in Caleb after only a few months with the Erudite; he dons glasses with false lenses to appear more in line with his new faction's aims, and he eventually takes his desire to fit in among the Erudite to the extreme by selling Tris out to Jeanine. This is deeply emblematic of gang brainwashing, or the hivemind, wherein "the activities of the gang become their normal functions. Others are viewed as outsiders and, at times, enemies. There is a lack of empathy toward others."[2]

---

[1] Savelli, Lou. "Behavior and Group Dynamics in Gangs." Gangs Blog, *Police Magazine*. 31 Aug. 2010. <http://www.policemag.com /blog/gangs/story/2010/08/gangs-behavior-and-group-dynamics /aspx>.

[2] Savelli, "Behavior and Group Dynamics in Gangs."

Finding parallels between the factions and *specific* gangs within today's Chicago is, unsurprisingly, not as easy. With so many active gangs in Chicagoland, looking at gang territories to determine faction homes was like picking through a real-life consequential haystack to find a fictional dystopian needle. There are crews all over the city who wear the Dauntless colors—black—and more who wear Erudite's blue, Amity's red and yellow, and even Abnegation's gray (Candor's black and white suits were not represented). And there was also no guarantee real-world gang colors had any influence on the factions' to begin with.

Instead, I looked to what concrete detail the books themselves provide, and Candor proved the easiest place to begin. Though we see the least of this faction in the novels, Candor helpfully provides us with some logistical truth (as their faction members would be proud to do): a set of directions in *Allegiant* from the Erudite compound to the Candor HQ. "We run in a pack down the alley towards Monroe Street," Tris narrates in *Allegiant*. "[W]e're on State Street [where it's] safe to talk . . . I use my watch light to see the words written on my arm. 'Randolph Street!'"

Of course, those directions could lead to dozens of buildings. Chicago's a big city. But that's where Candor's preference for suits and truth comes in, and so does a bit more of Chicago's sordid history—because Chicago isn't called the Windy City for the weather; instead, it refers to the reputation of the city's politicians for being "windbags"—their lack of candor (ahem), one might say. From the corruption of Senator William "Blond Boss" Lorimer in 1912 to the 1933 mob assassination of Mayor Anton Cermak to the fifty-year Daley Dynasty (during which the popular Chicago phrase "vote early and often" first came into use), Chicago has been a national hotbed of dirty politics for over a hundred years—probably a century more by Tris' lifetime. Where better for the faction dedicated to radical honesty to live than the Richard J. Daley Cultural Center, located on a convenient walking path from Monroe to State to Randolph, right across the river from the "Merciless Mart"?

The idea of Candor—anyone of candor—living under the name of Daley may even qualify as a Chicagoland inside joke, a nod to the deep corruption of Chicago's political past. The Daleys were a Democratic dynasty that ran the city from the early 1950s until 2011, at the time of *Divergent*'s release. While neither Mayor Daley—Richard J. or his son Richard M. Daley, who followed him to the mayoral seat—were officially charged with corruption themselves, many in their administration faced charges, as did other Illinois and Chicago-area officials during their reign. Not only does a shadow of dishonesty hang over the memory of Richard J. Daley, but the man was also known for his terrible habit of spoonerisms, mixing up his words in speeches and rallies. Indeed, quite contrary to Candor's beliefs, one aide to Daley is claimed to have told a reporter, "Report what he means, not what he says!"[3]

Reversing the directions from Candor headquarters that Uriah gives Tris during *Allegiant* leads back to Erudite's: a building that, we learn in *Divergent*, backs onto an alley on Monroe Street, less than a mile from Union Station, where the "Erudite live in large stone buildings that overlook the marsh." Tris tells us, "Across from Erudite headquarters is what used to be a park. Now we just call it 'Millennium.'" While on the trek to the Capture the Flag game, Tris can see the Bean and the other mammoth, electric-interactive statues. From Navy Pier, she can see Erudite's lights at night.

---

[3] Enright, L. *Chicago's Most Wanted: The Top 10 Book of Murderous Mobsters, Midway Monsters, and Windy City Oddities*. Dulles, VA: Potomac Books Inc., 2005.

Given that Erudite's ideology revolves around the acquisition and retention of knowledge, the first place that seemed possible as a headquarters was the Museum Campus, a cluster of stone buildings on the lakeshore that includes the Field Museum, the Adler Planetarium, and the Shedd Aquarium. The campus is, however, almost six miles from Union Station if Monroe, State, and Randolph are involved in travel—too far away from the other locations, such as Navy Pier and the Magnificent Mile, identified in the book. The Bean is also invisible from the campus' stone bridge. So where else in the city is a haven for learning?

Many places. Chicago is a cultural center in the United States, and Erudite might live in the Newberry Library, the University of Illinois at Chicago, the University of Chicago, the Museum of Science and Industry . . . or the Art Institute, a million-square-foot behemoth that includes its own affiliated school of the arts, permanent installations of artworks, and the capacity to hold 100,000 museum visitors. Located right on the edge of Millennium Park on Michigan and Monroe Avenues, right off the Red Line train, the Art Institute seemed the perfect place for Jeanine to conduct her research.

Further evidence the Art Institute may be Erudite headquarters? Describing a photo she posted on her blog in 2010, Veronica Roth wrote: "[I]n front of the lion statue in front of the Art Institute of Chicago. You may not have heard, but the Chicago Blackhawks won the Stanley Cup this year, and we're all very excited about it. Hence the huge Blackhawks helmet on the lion's head . . . So there you have it. A short tour through Chicago, and by proxy, through some of the scenes in DIVERGENT."[4]

---

[4] Roth, Veronica. "A Day In the Land of Divergent." Veronica Roth Blog. 22 June 2010. <http://veronicarothbooks.blogspot .com/2010/06/day-in-land-of -divergent.html>.

That run from Erudite to Candor in *Allegiant* is one of the only times in the series that Tris gets around Chicago purely by walking rather than taking the train. Since Chicago is the metropolitan center of the heartland, over 1,300 trains run through Chicago every day! From the long-distance Amtrak trains that seem likely to have been abandoned in Tris' fractured world to the suburban commuter train line of the Metra, trains are one of Chicago's most wide-ranging ways to travel.

Tris' trains, though, are almost certainly the el: a system of eight rapid-transit trains that spider through Chicago like the spokes of a wheel, with The Loop—home to Divergent's "Hub," the massive skyscraper at the center of the city that Tris tells us in *Divergent* is the Willis (Sears) Tower—as its center. The rest of Tris' world is so dependent on these trains—the paths between the factions running on train lines and the route to landmarks like the Hub and school accessible by train—that to make any further judgments of locations, the lines of the el needed to be added to the map.

Since Tris jumps off a train onto the roof of Dauntless headquarters, having placed the train routes should make it easier to now locate Dauntless. "The building I'm on forms one side of a square with three other buildings," Tris tells us in *Divergent*. "In the center . . . is a huge hole in the concrete." The Dauntless headquarters are also at least thirty minutes from the Hub, "far from the heart of the city," on the same train line as the Abnegation school trains, and possess a cavern big enough to be the Pit, as well as tunnels and an overhanging platform. That's a lot of specificity for a building that doesn't seem to match any in modern Chicago!

A popular fan theory is that the Dauntless sequester themselves in Thompson Center, a governmental building

for the state of Illinois. It is round and tall, easily accessible by Chicago's el trains, and encompasses enough land to make up a square city block. But the Thompson is not directly under the el—a jump like the Dauntless are fond of would be nearly impossible—and it is in The Loop, the base of Chicago's bustling downtown, located within minutes, even when walking, of the Hub. While the Thompson shares some characteristics with Dauntless' HQ, I wasn't satisfied with the idea of Tris, Tobias, and Tori living there.

The majority of buildings that the el trains would overhang closely enough to make the roof jump possible are in The Loop, the downtown area of the city where the biggest skyscrapers—like the Willis (Sears) Tower and Candor's Daley Cultural Center, among others—reign. Of course, none of these massive architectural feats could be the Dauntless headquarters itself, since jumping onto their roofs would take an airplane, not a train! Also, while "train tracks loop around the Dauntless compound," it is far from "the heart of the city" (*Divergent*). Tris tells us it takes thirty minutes (or more) to get to the Dauntless headquarters from the Hub by elevated train and that the tracks are seven stories high, at least, where the Dauntless make their rooftop jump. So that would take any buildings in, or near, The Loop out of the running.

Other places where trains loop around any buildings of significance are few and far between. There are some warehouses in the Lincoln Park area of the city; a few restaurants in the Gold Coast. Nowhere really seemed to match Tris' descriptions of the sprawling compound complete with a Pit and room for many shops and venues, like Tori's tattoo parlor.

One of the places that came to mind as a potential location is Chicago's historic shopping attraction, Water Tower Place. The octagonal free fall of the corridors and staircases called to mind the drop that Tris recounts making as

*Water Tower Place's shopping center,
named for (and located beside) the only surviving landmark of the Great Chicago Fire.*

she flies through the hole in the roof, and, of course, there
would be plenty of room to live, work, play, and train all in
one massive compound.

While there is no water in this "Water Tower Place"
anymore—the water tower itself is across the street, and
even that's become an art gallery—it wouldn't be a stretch to
imagine its insides gutted and retrofitted to include more natural rock formations and the treacherous Dauntless waterfall
where Al met his end. Also, it is located far from the "heart
of the city," although a walk from Dauntless to Erudite or
Navy Pier along the Magnificent Mile would be a snap for
the well-trained Dauntless warriors.

However, there are no train tracks that overhang its

roof. The closest stops let off four blocks away, and that's too large a leap for anyone, even someone with only six fears in the world.

Water Tower Place was out. Maybe placing Abnegation, since the Dauntless pass their row houses by train to get home from the Choosing Ceremony in *Divergent*, would help settle the location; they should be on the same line of Chicago's complicated, multispoked el.

The location of Abnegation is fairly concrete, although not as much as Candor's: When the Dauntless under simulation are sent to attack Abnegation's leaders, Tris recounts the mob's presence at the corner of North and Fairfield. That would put Abnegation in the Humboldt Park neighborhood of the city, historic home of the Roman Catholic Archdiocese of Chicago Our Lady of the Angels Catholic School, which burned in a tragic fire. Given the beliefs and dogma of Abnegation, as well as their adherence to rules similar to the Catholic vow of poverty and charity, the neighborhood seems like an appropriate one for Abnegation's home.

Like the members of Abnegation, the residents of today's Humboldt Park put a lot of time and energy into improving the city: in 1995, concerned citizens created the action group The United Blocks of West Humboldt Park (TUBOWHP), which aims to "enhance the livability of the area by establishing and maintaining an open line of communication and liaison between the neighborhood, government agencies and other neighborhoods" and "provide an open process by which all members of the neighborhood may involve themselves in the affairs of the neighborhood."[5]

---

[5] TUBOWHP. *United Blocks of West Humboldt Park*. Retrieved October 31, 2013, from United Blocks of West Humboldt Park: <http://unitedblocks.blogspot.com>.

The comparisons are not all positive ones. Sadly, like Abnegation's decimation by Jeanine's simulation, the area has long been a victim of the city's epidemic of violence. The Division Street Riots gripped the neighborhood in 1966, and in the late 1960s, 1970s, and 1980s, various street gangs—the Young Lords, the Latin Kings, the Spanish Cobras, the Latin Disciples—grappled for domination of the area. Eventually, the Young Lords, who originated in the Humboldt Park area—and wore Abnegation gray—teamed up with the neighborhood's government and community organizers to aid in the repairs of the neighborhood. They also took a stand for better protections for Puerto Rican citizens in Chicago, which may be alluded to through the Abnegation's work with the factionless in *Divergent*.[6]

Putting Abnegation's faction headquarters at the intersection of North and Fairfield sets it right at the City Colleges of Chicago's Humboldt Park Vocational Education Center of Wright College, an adult outreach school specializing in nursing—an appropriate place for Abnegation, who focus so much on helping others. There are also Catholic churches in the vicinity from where the faction could be led. The Vocational Education Center is accessible by the el's Blue Line train, so Tris, Caleb, and, once upon a time, Tobias could have taken this route from Humboldt Park to the big multifaction school in The Loop.

However, we can't use the Blue Line to guess at Dauntless' headquarters location. We know that the Dauntless ride a different path to school than the Abnegation since Tris, when she was Beatrice, would wait and watch them

---

[6] Judson Jefferies, "From Gang-Bangers to Urban Revolutionaries: The Young Lords of Chicago." *Journal of the Illinois State Historical Society* 96 (2003).

disembark from their own train every day at school: "I pause by a window in the E Wing and wait for the Dauntless to arrive. I do this every morning. At exactly 7:25, the Dauntless prove their bravery by jumping from a moving train" (*Divergent*). While Tris passes the Abnegation neighborhood on her way to Dauntless HQ after the Choosing Ceremony, the two trains are certainly on different lines—different paths—and intersect primarily at the school.

The school in the series is primarily noted for its "large metal sculpture" (*Divergent*). There is no shortage of these in Chicago; in The Loop alone, there are roughly twenty! The largest and most recognizable are the "The Picasso" and Calder's "Flamingo," both of which are large, metal, and sit in front of buildings. Schools that have statues are a part of Chicago's landscape as well, such as the the University of Chicago campus, but its main statue is stone—and it sits well outside The Loop area where Tris' school is suggested to be.

The most likely place for Tris' school is the Harold Washington Library Center, set in The Loop and flanked by massive copper gargoyles, within spitting distance of the large red metal Flamingo.

The Flamingo, a familiar
Chicago landmark that
practically begs for some
Dauntless climbing.

*The Harold Washington Library.
Its cornices also include statues
of owls, which are symbols of
knowledge—ideal for a school!*

Even with Abnegation, Candor, and Erudite placed—
and of course knowing the locations of landmarks that
Tris' Chicago shares with our own, such as Navy Pier—I
wasn't sure where Dauntless was meant to be. The University of Chicago campus still seemed workable, but just too
far south. Maybe mapping out the farthest borders of Tris'
city would help: time to turn to Amity.

I don't envy the Amity's commute to school every day!
Tris mentions in *Allegiant* that on the path from Amity's compound to the outside, Tris' group of Allegiant walk along
Route 90. In Chicago en route to O'Hare Airport, this would
mean I-90—locally called the Kennedy Expressway—a highway that, in modern times, is so prone to congestion that it
strikes terror in the hearts of commuters. Traffic updates are
broadcast on local radio stations and to websites every eight
minutes or less, and, despite being a high-speed expressway,

speeds average twenty miles per hour or less. (One can only assume that congestion would improve after the population thinned in the "Purity War," though, so maybe the Amity are luckier than Chicagoans today.) The same Blue Line that would bring Abnegation to the school does follow along the line of the Kennedy Expressway, and is likely the same train that would bring the Amity students to the school and its workers to the Hub when needed.

Of course, the hallmark of Amity's home is not what road it lies on, but the fact that it is comprised largely of farmland, which means that it needs to lie outside the boundaries of the metropolitan city center. While the outlying areas of Chicagoland abound with forest preserves, orchards, and other areas of agriculture, Tris doesn't recount passing through any other green spaces on her way to Amity from the other factions or when traveling from the edge of Amity into the fearsome territory outside the fence. Finding a place where Amity might be able to farm and live in space fundamentally different to the city interior—but which still fell along I-90 on the Kennedy—meant that the most likely place for Amity's meeting hall would be the Donald E. Stephens Convention Center, just off the Catherine Chevalier Woods in Rosemont, a near-suburb of the city.

With 8,137 acres of arable natural space that includes the banks of the Des Plaines River (for the hydroponics Tris sees in use while a refugee at the Amity campground) and a floodplain that lends itself to natural regrowth of prairie vegetation, the Catherine Chevalier Woods seem like a fitting place for Amity to have made their home. However, another possible location is a forest preserve and park only five miles up the road, still along the Kennedy Expressway: Caldwell Woods, named for Billy Caldwell, chief of the Potawatomi Indians. Caldwell is known in local Chicago history for saving the lives of an important Chicago political family

Greater Chicago

Bahaii Temple

Wilmette

Northwestern University

Evanston

Morton Grove

Skokie

14

41

Niles

Edison Park

Lincolnwood

Rogers Park

LAK

MICHI

Park Ridge

Smith Forest Preserve

Norwood Park

90

Jefferson Park

14

Loyola University

Chicago Internat Airport

AMITY

Schiller Woods

Norridge

Harwood Heights

Irving Park

Uptown

41

Lincoln Park

Schiller Park

Dunning

Portage Park

90

Avondale

Wrigley Field

Belmont Harb

Franklin Park

River Grove

Belmont Cragin

Logan Square

Old Town

Lincoln Park Zoo

Elmwood Park

Maywood Park Race Track

thlake

Stone Park

River Forest

Oak Park

Austin

West Town

ABNEGATION

Gold Coast

John Han

Melrose Park

Bellwood

Frank Lloyd Wright Home

Garfield Park

United Center

Near North

Downtown Chicago

he

Chica Harb

Maywood

290

Univ. of Illinois of Chicago

Instit Grant

Field Mu

Adle

Soldier

Broadview

Miller Meadow

Forest Park

Douglas Park

Cicero

Chinatown

CHI

stchester

Chicago Zoological Park

North Riverside

Berwyn

Lawndale

Bridgeport

Burn Harb

La Grange Park

Riverside

34

55

Comiskey Park

Illinois Inst of Tech

4

Brookfield

Lyons

Stickney

Forest View

McKinley Park

Brighton Park

Bu

A.E. Stevenson Expwy.

Grange

McCook

Sherman Park

Washington Park

Hyd Par

Countryside

Summit

Gage Park

Chicago Lawn

Ogden Park

Univ. of Chicago

Ja

Chicago Midway Airport

Bedford Park

Englewood

55

Hodgkins

Marquette Park

90

dian ead ark

Bridgeview

Hayford

Ashburn

Chatham

294

during the Fort Dearborn Massacre—an act certainly compatible with Amity's belief in harmony, but perhaps more suited to Abnegation's altruistic selflessness. Because the Catherine Chevalier Woods are larger and closer to O'Hare Airport, however, they seem a more fitting home for the Amity faction than Caldwell Woods.

Before the revelation that Amity was en route to O'Hare Airport, it seemed likely that their compound actually fell on the other side of the city, where Chicago's I-90 leads into Indiana. The methods and tenets of Amity seem in line with the idea of the Amish, who have populations in central and southern Illinois, Iowa, and Indiana, but none in Chicago itself or its immediate surrounding area. It's possible that they are intended to be Quaker or Mennonite in origin as well, but the only Quaker Society of Friends meetinghouses in the city fall on the extreme South Side, far from everywhere else referenced in the series and inaccessible via the train lines the other factions rely on.

So with four out of five factions solidly located, the sticky issue of Dauntless' overhanging trains and "thirty-minute" distance from The Loop via public transit comes back into play. It seems unlikely that it would be on the far South Side, since that would be a broader net of surveillance for the Bureau, with Amity and Abnegation up North; plus, three of the four other factions are accessible by Blue Line or Red Line. If we assume Dauntless headquarters is similarly located, it narrows the field of possibilities to the areas of Chicagoland north of Congress Parkway and the Eisenhower Expressway and west of State Street. Since Tris recounts passing the Abnegation row houses on her way to Dauntless' headquarters when she first leaves the Choosing Ceremony, we also know that Dauntless must be located in the north.

There is another line of trains that runs in this

Greater Chicago

Bahaíi Temple
Wilmette
DAUNTLESS
Northwestern University
Evanston

Morton Grove
Skokie
41

Niles

Edison Park

Lincolnwood
Rogers Park

14

Park Ridge

Norwood Park
Smith Forest Preserve
41

Loyola University

LA
MICH

Chicago International Airport
90
Jefferson Park

AMITY
Schiller Woods

Harwood Heights
Irving Park
Uptown

Norridge

Schiller Park

Dunning
Portage Park
90
Avondale

Lincoln Park

Wrigley Field
Belmont Harb

Franklin Park
River Grove
Belmont Cragin
Logan Square

Old Town
Lincoln Park Zoo

Elmwood Park

Maywood Park Race Track
thlake

Stone Park
River Forest
Oak Park
Austin
West Town

ABNEGATION

Gold Coast
John Har

Melrose Park

Bellwood
Frank Lloyd Wright Home
Garfield Park
United Center
Near North
Downtown Chicago
Chic Harb

Insti

Maywood
200

Univ. of Illinois of Chicago
Grant Field M
Adl
oldier

Broadview
Forest Park
Douglas Park
CH

Miller Meadow
Cicero
Chinatown
Burn Harb

stchester

Chicago Zoological Park
North Riverside
Berwyn
Lawndale
Bridgeport
Illinois Ins of Tech

La Grange Park
Riverside
34
55
Comiskey Park
Bu

Stickney
McKinley Park

Brookfield
Lyons
Forest View
Brighton Park

a Grange
A.E. Stevenson Expwy.

McCook
Sherman Park
Washington Park
Hyd
Par

Countryside
Summit
Gage Park
Univ. of Chicago
Ja

Chicago Midway Airport
Chicago Lawn
Ogden Park

dian ead ark
Bedford Park
Englewood

Hodgkins
Marquette Park
90

55
Bridgeview
Hayford

294
Ashburn
Chatham

14
45
34

Greater Chicago

Bahaii Temple
Wilmette
Northwestern University
Evanston

DAUNTLESS

Morton Grove
Skokie

14

41

Des Plaines

Niles

Lincolnwood

Edison Park

Rogers Park

Loyola University

Park Ridge

Smith Forest Preserve

14

90

Norwood Park

Jefferson Park

41

Harwood Heights

Irving Park

Uptown

Chicago Internat. Airport

AMITY

Schiller Woods

Norridge

Lincoln Park

90

Schiller Park

Dunning

Portage Park

Avondale

Wrigley Field

Belmont H

294

Franklin Park

River Grove

Belmont Cragin

Logan Square

Old Town

Lincoln Park Zoo

Maywood Park Race Track

Elmwood Park

Northlake

Stone Park

River Forest

Oak Park

Austin

West Town

Gold Coast

John H

Melrose Park

ABNEGATION

Near North

Downtown Chicago

Bellwood

Frank Lloyd Wright Home

Garfield Park

United Center

41

Maywood

290

Forest Park

Douglas Park

Univ. of Illinois of Chicago

Chinatown

Broadview

Miller Meadow

Cicero

Westchester

North Riverside

Berwyn

Lawndale

Bridgeport

Illinois I of Tech

Chicago Zoological Park

Comiskey Park

34

Riverside

55

La Grange Park

Stickney

McKinley Park

Washington Park

34

Brookfield

Lyons

Forest View

Brighton Park

Univ. of Chicago

La Grange

McCook

Sherman Park

Countryside

Summit

Gage Park

Chicago Lawn

Ogden Park

Englewood

Indian Head Park

Hodgkins

55

Chicago Midway Airport

Bedford Park

Marquette Park

90

294

Bridgeview

Ashburn

Hayford

Chatha

A.E. Stevenson Expwy.

LA MICH

quadrant, on a specialized route to somewhere that Veronica Roth may have, in her own life, seen as a symbol of courage: the Purple Line train runs to Northwestern University, where she wrote *Divergent*.

The train doesn't overhang any of the buildings here, but the Northwestern campus does share features with the rest of Dauntless headquarters' setting: the dome of the Dearborn Observatory and the cluster of interconnected buildings are certainly enough space to live, work, and play all in one place. It's entirely possible that Northwestern University is the home of the Dauntless, not because it's a logistical match to the descriptions in the novels—it isn't—but because of what the school may have become emblematic of for Roth back when the idea of the factions and the story of the Divergent trilogy were first conceived. When Roth chose to transfer colleges and enter Northwestern's notoriously rigorous program, when she wrote *Divergent* over winter break and shopped the manuscript during term—her actions took guts. Perhaps, even, a leap of faith, not unlike Beatrice's transformation into Tris with a flying jump onto the roof of her unknown new home.

V. Arrow *is the author of Smart Pop's The Panem Companion and an essay about Real Person Fanfiction in the Smart Pop anthology* Fic. *She sometimes gives speeches and presentations about related topics at conferences, conventions, and schools. The rest of the time, she blogs a lot about boy band and YA lit topics and writes both original young adult fiction and fanfiction. If she lived in Tris' world, she would probably choose Erudite, minus all of the evil.*

One of the great things about science fiction is its ability to work in metaphor—to take a real-world situation and remake it as something larger than life, rendering it at once both easier to understand and more epic.

Take Divergent's *Choosing Ceremony. The choice of factions in Tris' world comes at the same age many teenagers in ours are facing an important decision: what to do after high school graduation. In our world, we express our choice through things like applications rather than ritual bloodletting in front of family and friends, but emotionally, the declaration can feel just as serious, and just as public. Will you go to college, the way an Erudite might? Join the military, like the Dauntless?*

Here, mother and daughter Maria V. Snyder and Jenna Snyder discuss college, career, and what the Divergent trilogy has to say about making life's big choices.

CHOICES CAN BE MADE AGAIN

MARIA V. SNYDER AND JENNA SNYDER

MARIA

Recently, my daughter Jenna turned sixteen, and our household has been discussing her future career choice and where she'd like to attend college. As a high school sophomore, Jenna is facing a big decision just like *Divergent*'s sixteen-year-old protagonist Tris, who had to choose a faction.

JENNA

In the beginning of *Divergent*, Tris knows she has to make a huge choice once she turns sixteen: go to the Choosing Ceremony and decide, in front of everyone, which faction she will join. This is similar to my choice of where to attend college after high school and what career to pursue, though mine involves a lot less pressure. I can always pick something else if things don't work out or if I change my mind. Tris has one chance. She has to make that one choice count, and that's really scary.

MARIA

Early on in *Divergent*, Tris takes an aptitude test to discover which of the five factions she belongs in. Her test results indicate an aptitude for multiple factions, though most people in her society are a fit for just one. As a student who has to decide on a career path and college within the next couple years, would you like to be able to take a test and have it decided for you?

JENNA

The idea of being able to take a test and have all my difficult choices decided for me sounds great at first. However, I've actually experienced such tests, although they weren't quite so advanced as the ones in *Divergent*, and I've noticed a number of flaws.

There is a career site, called Career Cruising, my school guidance program uses to help kids decide on a career. It asks you questions about your interests and skills and then generates a list of careers you might be interested in, graded on how well your skills suggest you would do in them. Sounds straightforward, but at the moment I aspire to be a journalist, and although my interests put it on my list, my skill answers ranked it a C. I strongly disagree.

Actually, Career Cruising did not give an A to any of the careers that matched my interests. Is it trying to tell me I won't be good at any job that I would enjoy? That doesn't make sense. Some of the careers I scored a B for were market research analyst, translator, and researcher, but I'm not interested in any of them. It's like how Tris showed aptitude for Abnegation and Erudite in addition to Dauntless. She could have done well in either Abnegation or Erudite, because her skills were a match, but neither would have been a good fit for her, just like researcher wouldn't be a good fit for me. Neither of us would excel as well as we would in another faction or career because we wouldn't love it.

MARIA

I can understand why market research analyst and researcher scored higher for you. You are logical and practical, you like order (except in your room), and you have the spark of creativity needed to bring all those skills together. But I agree, sometimes desire is as important as ability. Maybe that's why Tris' city has a Choosing Ceremony, not an Announcing Ceremony. No one is forced to pick the faction he or she shows the most aptitude for. We learn in the side story *The Transfer* that Tobias' test showed his aptitude was for Abnegation (though, admittedly, he was able to influence the results thanks to Marcus' training), yet he chose Dauntless.

And of course, Tris chooses Dauntless. It's who she wants to be, not her abilities, that ends up being most important to her. Living with the Abnegation all her life, she's had no experience with jumping on a moving train or leaping off a building. Yet she is determined to do well in her new faction, and she does. She persists and refuses to give up even after being beaten by Peter and almost tossed into the chasm.

Then again, if she hadn't been *any* good at being

Dauntless, she wouldn't have made it through initiation, no matter how much she wanted to belong there. Do you worry about not having the right skills or talent to be a journalist and "washing out"?

JENNA

Occasionally I worry that I am not a good enough writer to pursue a career in journalism. There are declining job openings, and it can get quite competitive. I will always have doubts about whether I will be successful, but I know that I work hard in everything that I do and will put forth my best work. I believe these qualities will ultimately lead me to find a great job.

MARIA

In *Divergent*, Tris' parents aren't allowed to discuss the test or the results, and I think there are some benefits to parents not offering their opinion. It means there is no pressure for their children to please them and they can look deep within themselves and discover what their true desires are. But you already know that, when I think of careers for you, I lean toward librarian or teacher.

Would it have been better if I hadn't offered any advice or opinions? Would you find it helpful to make these kinds of decisions entirely on your own?

JENNA

I know that some kids don't have the benefit of understanding parents, and some of my friends are not as free to go against their parents' wishes as I am, but I feel like even if I don't always agree with you, I value your opinion (most of the time).

You're right that librarian and teacher would fit me better in some ways, since I'm good at interacting with people. However, neither of those options appeal to me as much as journalism—where being personable would also help in doing interviews—as I would have to work with kids and do clerical work, which I'm not interested in *at all*.

Even when I disagree with you, I would never make a permanent choice like Tris' before talking to you and Dad and even some of my friends. In making a big decision like that, I would *want* to discuss it with my family and friends. And I think not talking about my decisions could lead me to make worse ones. I might be more hesitant to do something that might be beneficial for me just because I'm not totally comfortable with it, like when I considered trying out for the soccer team. I was worried that I'd missed too much of the preseason and that I'd feel left out around the other girls, but after talking with you and my friends, I decided to try out and loved playing (go Bears!).

However, that's for big decisions. In small everyday choices I make about what clubs to join and how to do my projects, I think I'm better off with my opinion being the only one that matters. And in the end, it's my life, and if other people always make every decision for you, you will never be truly happy. Luckily, I'm a teenager, and even with your parental advice I still will probably not listen to you all the time and will do things to be different and independent. It's basically a rite of passage for every teen.

MARIA

Not listen to me all the time? Gasp! (Actually, I'm well aware of that, since you decided to play the screechy violin instead of the soothing cello, which I recommended.)

When Tris is deciding what faction to choose in *Divergent*, she rules out Erudite right away because that faction had spread vicious rumors about the Abnegation and because her father hates them. Tris feels loyalty for her faction and to her father, which does factor in her decisions. How can it not? She grew up in Abnegation, and her family and friends are all part of the faction. But Tris is still left deciding between Abnegation and Dauntless—two completely different factions. She can't choose both.

Looking back on my school years, I was torn between two very different options of my own—I was also Divergent. My best grades were in math and science. I especially enjoyed earth science and decided to become a meteorologist when I was in sixth grade. (Ironically, my grades in English and spelling were horrible and I hated writing. Yes, hated, loathed, avoided—take your pick.) At that time in my life, however, I also played the cello, and I danced, painted, and acted in all the school plays. I daydreamed of becoming a famous actress or dancer. I thought back then that I would have to choose between science and art.

In our society, we tend to view science and art as opposites, even though science suggests that the two are actually closely related; for instance, studies have shown that children who take piano lessons at an early age do better in math than those who don't. In Tris' society, they have separated their citizens based on individual aptitudes—intelligence, bravery, honesty, selflessness, and peacefulness. When Tris is debating between Abnegation and Dauntless, she's torn between selflessness and bravery. As the story progresses, though, she begins to understand that the two aspects are intertwined. Her selflessness, as Four says, makes her brave. By the end of *Allegiant*, she realizes her Abnegation values and her Dauntless bravery are one and the same.

Back then I chose science because I lacked confidence in my artistic abilities and felt I'd never "make it big." I worked as a meteorologist for ten years, and while some aspects of the job were interesting and challenging, I wasn't having much fun—unlike my current career as a fiction author (and essayist—hi, Mom!), where not only am I good at it, I'm having a blast.

I wonder what Career Cruising would have picked for me. Would I have gotten an A in fiction writing? Would I have saved time and money by concentrating on writing right away instead of studying meteorology? Or would I have ignored the advice? I probably would have ignored it. Scratch that: I *know* I'd have viewed the results as crazy. I wasn't as brave as Tris.

From your answers, Jenna, you could also be considered Divergent. You've always done well in English class, yet you're also enrolled in precalculus as a tenth grader and you tutor other students in your school in math. What draws you to journalism? Is it, like Tris, from a sense of loyalty or familiarity with the writing profession, since I am a writer?

JENNA

Ever since I was in middle school, I just knew that I wanted to take journalism classes in high school and write for the school newspaper. It just always was that way. I had no doubt. I believe my love of reading and writing is partly because of your profession, but journalism allows me to do something similar while writing about so many more fun and interesting topics than I'd be able to if I wrote books, the way you do. Thus it allows me to be an individual while still connecting back to you.

This isn't so different from Tris finding out her mother had come from Dauntless (though later we learn her mother came from outside the city), or finding out her father came from Erudite, especially since Erudite was the faction her brother, Caleb, chose. It suggests that both Caleb and Tris are more like their parents than they thought, even though they made their own different choices.

I do enjoy tutoring math. I like knowing I'm making a difference in someone's educational experience and, hopefully, making it better. However, I do not wish to pursue teaching math in the long term. Tutoring is just one way for me to help others and still get to enjoy math.

MARIA

Exploring what you enjoy doing is a wonderful way to "test the waters." In fact, attending college is a journey of discovery. In Tris' world, though, there's no trial period, no chance for her to see what each faction really does before she chooses where to spend the rest of her life. She has the results of her aptitude test, cultural knowledge of the factions, and the few interactions she's had with kids from other factions at school. Tris knows she is drawn to the Dauntless; she watches them jump off the trains every morning and she admits her gaze "cling[s] to them wherever they go." She also knows that her father calls them "hellions," which may trigger her natural teenage tendency to rebel against parental opinion. And she knows that she does not feel at home in Abnegation; she longs to feel free, and the Dauntless seem to be free. There are a number of things that play into her decision, just like there will be for you when you decide on a college and a career. But for Tris, once she chooses, there's no going back.

I can still remember when my older sister Karen wanted to be a pharmacist. She was accepted into the Philadelphia

College of Pharmacy, but then she worked part-time in a pharmacy and decided not to pursue it as a career because she was bored. I wanted to "test out" my future career as a tornado chaser, but my parents refused to drive me out West (can you believe that?). Tris doesn't have the same option. If, when she learns exactly what is involved in being Dauntless during her initiation period, she doesn't feel at home there, either, she can't just choose to try some other faction out instead. If she changes her mind, or can't cut it, she'll be factionless—way scarier than having an undeclared major.

You recently did a career-shadow with a working journalist at a local newspaper. How has that experience factored into your thoughts about being a journalist?

JENNA

Seeing how much they write and all the different people they meet and interview was a positive for me. I was also interested in the digital work involved in a newspaper, such as the website maintenance and the layout programs. The newspaper I shadowed at actually uses the same layout program as I do in my school. Plus, the atmosphere was professional but friendly, and I had some fun conversations.

There were a couple things that gave me some doubts, though. The major one everyone mentions is that it's a changing career industry and jobs are hard to find. Lots of newspapers are laying off reporters, and some are closing from lack of sales. Many newspapers are going online, though no one knows if that will create more or fewer jobs. I also learned how important it is to get internships and experience if I want to work in the field, which pressures me to decide whether it's something I want to pursue even sooner.

I still have to really consider the pros and cons as it gets closer to when I have to decide. In the end, it might not come down to which choice is most logical. I'll make the one that feels right to me, and I'm sure I'll still have a few misgivings. Tris weighs the pros and cons of which faction to choose, but she still has many doubts even after she decides.

MARIA

Sometimes our decisions have more to do with emotion than logic. There are a lot of factors that go into Tris' decision: aptitude, skill, desire, passion, a touch of rebellion . . . and family values.

During the Choosing Ceremony, Tris is in turmoil over her choice, but she believes Caleb is calm and assumes that he will choose Abnegation. However, he surprises her by choosing Erudite, and she views his choice as an act of betrayal. Not only does their father hate Erudite, but Tris hasn't yet made her choice, and if they both leave Abnegation, their parents will be alone.

When I was choosing a college, my sister Karen was in her third year at Drexel University for chemical engineering. I already knew I was interested in meteorology, and Drexel had an atmospheric science major, so I applied there . . . mainly because the thought of going to a familiar school and already knowing a group of people (my sister and her friends) was comforting. Plus, like Tris did when she rejected Erudite immediately, I made the decision from a sense of loyalty—Drexel was my sister's school and she'd been the first person in our immediate and extended family to attend college. Our entire family was excited (go Dragons!). Then, increasing the pressure, Drexel accepted me and offered me a scholarship.

I followed my sister's footsteps for many things through-out my childhood. I learned how to play the piano because she bugged our parents for lessons. She joined orchestra in high school, and four years later, I did as well. There are a number of other examples of me being a "copycat," and, for a while, it appeared I'd go to the same college, too.

My mother questioned my initial decision to attend Drexel even though it wasn't the best choice for me. I grew up in Philadelphia and didn't relish the thought of attend-ing a city school—I wished for wide-open spaces and fresh air, and Drexel was in the middle of Philadelphia. The atmospheric science major Drexel offered wasn't exactly what I'd desired, either. The only reason I could offer her was how familiar and safe Drexel felt. Karen had shared her experiences with me so I knew what to expect.

Once I realized the motive for my choice, I also realized it was *my* life, not Karen's. She'd never pressured me to fol-low her; I was doing it from my own fear of the unknown. Fear can be a strong motivator. Consider Four's decision to leave Abnegation because he wanted to escape his father, or Tris' fear of upsetting her parents at the Choosing Cer-emony, though she eventually chooses Dauntless despite it.

Luckily for me, I'd also applied to Pennsylvania State Uni-versity, which is one of the best undergraduate meteorology programs in the United States, and they'd accepted me as well.

Your brother Luke just went through the whole choosing-a-college gauntlet. He chose to attend Penn State—the same school your father and I attended. What do you think about his choice? You know we are very proud of our alma mater and, truthfully, excited Luke is attending Penn State (go Lions!). Do you feel any pressure to attend Penn State?

JENNA ——————————————————————————————

I'm glad Luke is attending Penn State. I like Penn State and have fun cheering on their football team. However, I feel a need to branch off and go somewhere that would be better for my needs. You, Dad, and Luke all majored in scientific and mathematical things, while I'm hoping to go to school for a writing or journalism major. I'll probably still apply to Penn State even though I don't feel any pressure to attend. I know you and Dad will support me no matter what.

MARIA ——————————————————————————————

You don't feel any pressure? Huh. Guess I need to be more obvious.

Actually, I do agree that Penn State might not be the best fit for you. I think a smaller school with a good writing program would work. Like, say, Seton Hill University, where I teach in the MFA program. Seton Hill has an excellent undergraduate program (hint, hint). But you don't seem as . . . enthusiastic about the school as I am.

JENNA ——————————————————————————————

Oh my gosh! Stop bringing up Seton Hill! I DO NOT want to go there. This is probably the hundredth time you have brought it up.

MARIA ——————————————————————————————

All right, I'll stop . . . maybe . . .

I understand you want to attend a school far enough away that you have to live on campus. What drives this desire? Leaving home for college isn't the same as Tris choosing Dauntless and having to leave the only home she's ever known to go live with strangers, but it's still a gigantic step. I avoided leaving home for two years by attending a branch campus of Penn State before living at the main campus. Easing into the transition worked for me—I made a bunch of friends at the branch campus who moved with me.

JENNA

I enjoy having responsibility and doing things for myself, and I feel like when I'm a senior in high school I'll be ready to be on my own (and get away from the family—no offense, Mom). I make friends quickly, so I'm not worried about being alone my first year at college. I feel that being away from home will give me a chance to figure things out on my own. Also, it will force me to do things myself and without help from you and Dad. The freedom of college appeals to me, and I think I'll do well in that setting.

Still, even though I want to live on campus, I also want to live close enough that I can come back and enjoy the comforts of home every once in a while.

MARIA

You will always be welcome to come back home as long as you don't bring your dirty laundry for me to clean. And I plan to come visit you . . . often.

Tris' faction choice may be permanent, but her family is still allowed to visit—once, at least, and it's very similar to a parents' weekend at college. Tris' mother's visit during initiation helps Tris feel better about her decision because it means Natalie supports her daughter's choice. (Tris' father's absence also sends a clear message: he's upset by her choice.) It's also during that scene that her mother inadvertently reveals she was in Dauntless before choosing Abnegation, and knowing she has some family connection to the faction eases Tris' worries.

I remember when my parents helped me move into a dorm room for the first time. I couldn't wait for them to leave. After a few weeks on my own, I couldn't wait for them to come back! I remained on campus until Thanksgiving, and by that time, I *needed* to be home. In fact, when my friend's car died after she picked me up, I cried over the delay (while she cried over the cost of the repair). The desire to be home in my own bed surrounded by my family pulsed in my chest. It was a physical ache.

At one point, Tris feels the same way. She visits Caleb to pass on their mother's message about researching the simulation serum, but the desire to see him—to make a connection with a piece of home—also drives her actions. During the visit, though, she realizes that, even in the short time period they were apart, they have both changed and grown. Their differences are now glaringly obvious. Tris also understands "home" would never be the same. You may find the same is true after you go off to college.

Jenna

I'm sure when I come home from college, my room, the house, you and Dad, and the cat will all be the same, but I will feel different. Going away to college is a huge decision no matter if I go an hour away or five hours away from home. It's bound to change my life. Any big decision is.

Maria

I remember believing that my choice in careers would be the BIGGEST decision ever. And, once made, it'd be unchangeable. Thinking about all the money I'd spend for tuition and all the time I'd spend studying, I felt this choice would guide my entire life. Is that how you feel?

JENNA

I have a strong desire to make a good choice on my career and fully commit to it so I can find the best job I can, one that I'll enjoy. My friends and I feel the same way—that this is a big choice and we NEED to get it right. However, I know that you completely changed careers and now have a great job that you enjoy, and that it didn't matter that you didn't pick it to start with. Too bad my mind refuses logic. I'm already planning a career that I want to do for the rest of my life.

MARIA

My first month as a working meteorologist—doing air-quality assessments, sitting in a cubicle, and listening to my new coworkers complain—was horrible. I felt a little like Tris must have at the beginning of her initiation into Daunt-less: I thought I'd made the biggest mistake of my life. Then there were the office politics and the cliques. Tris has her own set of politics to suffer through. The other initiates form cliques and call her a Stiff, and, as the smallest initiate, she feels her odds of passing "are not good." Like me, she was also scared that she'd made a mistake.

What I didn't understand at the time was that I needed to adjust my visions of a perfect career and work environ-ment to be more realistic, just like Tris has to do when she joins Dauntless. She adjusts, works hard, refuses to give up despite almost being killed, and makes a couple friends.

Along the way, she learns to love her faction and proves she belongs there both to herself and to the others.

While I worked as a meteorologist, I found acceptance, but I also started writing. My transition to novelist spanned eight years as my hobby turned into a career. I returned to college, this time earning a Masters of Arts degree in writing from Seton Hill University (go Griffins!), and went on to publish twelve novels and a dozen short stories.

In today's world, my career change is hardly unique. According to a study by New York University researchers, a professional worker will, on average, change careers three times in a lifetime . . . which brings me to the crux of this conversation.

In *Insurgent*, Tobias' mother, Evelyn, wants him to join her and the factionless. Tobias reminds her he *chose* Dauntless, and she tells him that "choices can be made again." This quote resonated deeply with me. Not because she was trying to change his mind (go Dauntless!), but because it's true. You may not be able to change your original choice, but you can always make another one—a different one. And that takes the pressure off making the perfect choice. Because most of the time, there are no irreversibly bad ones—even in Tris' world.

My experiences, my education, my mistakes, my failures, my successes, the hours of hard work, and, yes, the hours of goofing off have culminated in who I am *right now*. I can't undo any of those choices I made. And truthfully I wouldn't.

If a test had told me to be a fiction writer when I was in high school, and I listened to it, I wouldn't have sparked on the idea that led to my second series of books about magicians who can harvest energy from storms and bottle it in glass orbs. I wouldn't have had the technical knowledge about the environmental systems needed to keep my characters alive while living in their giant metal cube in *Inside Out*. The examples are endless. I've learned life is fodder for my stories. No experience is wasted. And the perfect example of this is Tris' return to her Abnegation values. All her experiences as Dauntless, and all the difficulties she overcomes during the course of the three books of the Divergent trilogy, are what bring her to the decision to sacrifice herself at the end of *Allegiant*. They are why she knows it is the right thing to do.

That is why I told you that there is no wrong choice when it comes to picking a career or college. I remember you looked at me like I was crazy. And now's your chance to tell me why.

JENNA

The whole applications process with college is a big deal and to pick a college that doesn't fit you after going through all that would be horrible. If you choose a terrible college that has bad classes where you don't learn, it could prevent you from getting a good job. Your career is a big part of your life—you do it every day—and it's important to get it right.

Teenagers go through a lot of stress and work hard to get good grades while still having a social life and enough sleep (which we never get). We don't want all our hard work to be lost to a bad college or career because we feel like once we are on the path, it's a done deal.

Even if that isn't true, I still don't want to choose the wrong job for me and have to go through the process of changing everything—starting all over again, maybe even going back to school. It's a scary thing.

Change always has mystery to it. Tris didn't know

what she'd be entering into when she chose Dauntless. She hoped it would be a good change. But it also could have been a very bad one.

Maria

I understand and remember experiencing that worry and stress. There is nothing I can say that will alter your need to find the perfect college and career. And that's fine. Time and experience are wonderful teachers.

But I loved what you said about change. *Change always has mystery to it.* You're right. It invokes a whole laundry list of feelings—anxiety, fear, anticipation, and excitement. And it's our choices that create change. You can see this happen throughout the Divergent trilogy, but especially in *Allegiant*: Tobias choosing to give his mother a second chance and ending the impending war as a result; Tris choosing to sacrifice herself to erase the memories of the people living in the Bureau of Genetic Welfare in an attempt to rid the world of prejudice, and through that, freeing her city to live differently. Their choices allow many others to choose where and how to live their own lives.

So here's to making choices. I've no doubt you'll make the right one, Jenna (even if I may not agree with you!).

Meteorologist turned novelist Maria V. Snyder *has been writing since 1995. Eighteen years, twelve published novels, a dozen short stories, and a half-dozen awards later, Maria's learned a thing or three about writing. Her Study series (*Poison Study, Magic Study, *and* Fire Study*) has been on the* New York Times *bestseller list. Maria earned her Master of Arts degree from Seton Hill University where she's been teaching in their MFA program, which is why she would choose Erudite: she loves learning about new things and doing research for her novels.*

Jenna Snyder *is currently a sophomore in high school. She is on the school soccer team and is involved in the ski club. She plays the flute and violin in her school's band and orchestra. Reading and writing are two of the things Jenna enjoys most, and she has published book reviews in* MIZZ *magazine and an article, "Why Hurricanes Have Names," in the appendix of Maria V. Snyder's* Storm Watcher. *She is also on the staff of her school newspaper as an editor. She would choose Erudite because she enjoys learning about new topics and having intellectual conversation and discussions.*

During the scene in Divergent *where Tris takes Al's place in front of the target, Eric and Tobias argue about what it means to be Dauntless—what it means to be brave. Tobias says that "a brave man acknowledges the strength of others." Eric insists that "a brave man never surrenders." But Tris serves as a silent example of yet another understanding of bravery: a brave man (or woman) stands up for those who cannot do so for themselves.*

It's this third definition that the Divergent trilogy appears to take as its primary one; by its end, Tris has sacrificed herself to defend the rights (and memories) of her city's people, and Tobias has found meaning in similar sacrifice, as a politician working for change in the freer city that takes the Chicago experiment's place. But Elizabeth Norris suggests there is even more to bravery, and that Dauntless is not the only place to find it.

ORDINARY ACTS OF BRAVERY

ELIZABETH NORRIS

When I first read *Divergent*, it was a Saturday. I had a day of data entry in front of me and planned to reward myself with a chapter every few hours. As you might imagine, I didn't manage to stop after a chapter—or even a few chapters. I read *Divergent* in its entirety, only stopping once to send a quick DM to Veronica Roth, who I'd met on her recent trip to New York.

I told her that I desperately wanted to run outside, scream, "Dauntless!", and perhaps punch someone in the face. (Someone who deserved it, of course.) It was probably the highest form of flattery I could offer her, and thankfully, she took it as such. I loved the book so much that I felt inspired to turn into some kind of Dauntless superhero. That reckless feeling only lasted briefly (I'd be a terrible vigilante), but long after I had finished the novel, something else still lingered in the back of my mind.

I felt inspired to be brave.

Not that the book made me want to run into a burning building and save someone or enlist in the military (both of which require incredible courage and dedication), but I took a look at my own life, at the everyday normalcy of it, and wanted to find my own ordinary acts of bravery. Which is fitting, considering that when Veronica signs copies of *Divergent*, she writes, "Be brave."

It's clearly a theme that comes up a lot throughout the book. From the very first page, Tris is forced to act outside of her comfort zone; to face uncertainty, fear, and danger; and to make decisions that will change her life. But Tris isn't brave just because of the decision she makes at the Choosing Ceremony; it isn't because Tris chooses Dauntless that she becomes brave. As a true Divergent, she has personality traits that can be attributed to each of the five factions. Each of them, in their own right, make her brave.

ACTING IN SPITE OF FEAR

It's easy to see how Dauntless embodies bravery. It's what their faction stands for, part of their manifesto. They believe in bravery, in taking action, and in freedom from fear. However, it's the latter—the idea of acting in spite of fear—that their faction uses to define bravery.

We see that from the moment Tris chooses Dauntless. When the Choosing Ceremony is over, Tris and the other Dauntless initiates must run out of the building and to the train tracks. Their first test as part of their initiation is to jump onto the moving train, then jump from the train to the roof of Dauntless headquarters upon their arrival. The train is moving just fast enough that jumping onto it is possible, but requires a certain amount of physical strength and agility. Anyone who is out of shape or sick or even suffering from a physical disability would have a hard time passing this test. In effect, it's designed to weed out initiates who are physically weak right from the beginning. But there's more to it than just that. Jumping on and off the train leaves no room for hesitation. There is a specific window of time, as the train passes the roof, when the initiates must jump. Then, from their train car, they can see people in front of them jumping off when their turn comes. They can see the consequence if they fail, and all of them are afraid. The test, however, doesn't allow for that fear to control them. Even the slightest hesitation—*from fear*—could delay their jump, and anyone who jumps too late risks falling to his or her death.

The tests, of course, don't end once Tris and the other initiates arrive at Dauntless. On the roof they're immediately faced with another test: they're asked to jump down a hole without being able to see the bottom. Tris can tell it's at least several stories high, but that's all she knows. While this test is different from the train jump, it has one striking similarity. Again, its purpose is to see that the initiates are capable of freeing themselves from fear or at least acting in spite of it. This time, the fear stems partly from the unknown. The initiates, especially Tris, who volunteers to go first, must trust the Dauntless leaders and jump into this dark hole and fall despite the fact that they don't know where they will land. It is essentially a blind leap of faith where the initiates must banish all fear from their minds and trust that they will be okay. That this comes immediately after a Dauntless-born initiate misses the jump from the train to the roof and falls to her death, proving that no one is safe, only amplifies the potential consequences of this test, as well as the others they will face.

While the initiates are tested physically (physical training), they are tested emotionally (simulations) and mentally (fear landscapes), as well. As Tris mentions, in Dauntless they teach you to be completely self-reliant, to be prepared for anything, in order to minimize the fear in any given situation, which often means doing things the hard way. "There's nothing especially brave about wandering dark streets with no flashlight, but [Dauntless] are not supposed to need help, even from light" (*Divergent*). That preparation makes sense, especially given their role in the government—to protect the city. Similar to our own military preparations, Dauntless life is designed to make them capable of anything, so that when they're in a situation where there is no light, and they can only rely on themselves, there will also be no fear.

It also can make them foolhardy at times. Beating each other senseless in physical training, as the initiates are encouraged to do, and hanging over the chasm to prove one isn't a coward, as Christina is forced to do, are not actions that stem from bravery. In fact, they're more for cruelty's sake than bravery's.

Similarly, after Al's suicide, Eric praises him, and instead of a somber funeral, the Dauntless celebrate his "bravery" for going to a place unknown. We know that Al wasn't brave. He didn't choose to jump into the chasm in order to face the unknown. He wasn't cut out for Dauntless life. In fact, he was weak. Not because he kept missing the target in knife throwing and not because he needed Tris to take his place at the target. He was weak because he felt threatened by Tris' strength and allowed Peter to threaten her. Rather than stand up for her, like she did for him, he even helped Peter and Drew assault her and dangle her over the edge of the chasm.

By celebrating bravery that we know Al didn't have, Dauntless exposes a flaw in its definition of the concept. They're striving for "freedom from fear," but fearlessness is not always the same as bravery. Al's suicide might have indirectly proved that he didn't fear the ultimate unknown—death—but it was still an act of cowardice. For Al, the chasm was easier than facing the cutthroat aspects of Dauntless life and the shame he felt for his actions.

Fear isn't an enemy of bravery. Driving people to free themselves completely from fear doesn't necessarily mean their actions will be brave. Fear is what makes people brave—feeling afraid, yet acting in spite of that fear.

STANDING UP FOR ONE ANOTHER

When I first started thinking about the meaning of bravery in the world of Divergent, I had a hard time with Amity. I knew what I believed and what I wanted to prove—true bravery can be found in kindness—but even to my own ears that didn't sound like something other people would easily swallow. It was when I began to reread *Divergent* and *Insurgent* to prepare myself for *Allegiant*'s release that I realized that the connection between Amity and bravery is obvious. The decision to be kind even when faced with cruelty is brave.

The line from the Dauntless manifesto, "We believe in ordinary acts of bravery, in the courage that drives one person to stand up for another," is not actually practiced in Dauntless anymore, something that Will and Tris realize during initiation after Edward is stabbed in the eye (*Divergent*). In any other faction, it would be brave for them to report what had happened to Edward, to come forward and stand up for him by telling the truth, but in Dauntless coming forward will make them seem afraid. The bravery to stand up for another person is rooted in the virtue of Amity.

It isn't the absence of fear that makes Tris stand up for Al in *Divergent*, it's her kindness. She cares for Al, and she doesn't enjoy seeing him berated, first because he's struggling to throw a knife and hit the target and then because he's honest enough to admit that he's afraid of getting hit. Then when Eric orders Al to stand in front of the target, it's Tris' kindness that drives her to stand up to Eric and say, "Stop!"

Tris' kindness is often intertwined with her selflessness (more on this later, trust me), and her decision to take Al's place in front of the target can be attributed to both virtues. Eric makes the offer, and her instinct to accept it is selfless. She knows she can prevent Al from experiencing more pain and embarrassment by taking that on herself. But protecting him also makes Tris feel strong and brave—she feels like she belongs in Dauntless. As a result, it's not completely unselfish. But it's still kind. Tris is able to stand at the target and keep from flinching because she knows that it's the right thing to do—be kind and stand up for Al, who isn't as strong as she is. That's what makes her brave.

It is the same mix of kindness and selflessness that ultimately saves Tris' life in *Insurgent*. She saves Peter's life at the Amity compound. It's an instinct rather than a presence of mind that pushes her to dive into the Erudite woman pointing a gun. Tris acts without knowing the intended target because to her that doesn't matter. She knows she can stop someone from getting shot without any danger to herself, and she steps up to protect anyone she can. As a result the shot goes wide, hitting the wall instead of hitting Peter. He and Tris have never been friends. In fact, between his disparaging comments, threats of violence, and physical attacks, he's been cruel to her countless times. Their relationship is so strained, he doesn't thank her and she doesn't acknowledge him. Yet, Tris knows she saved his life and she doesn't regret it. She's capable of being kind to him despite his cruelty. Again, this instinct is both kind and selfless.

Later, when Peter is one of her captors, Tris further demonstrates her innate kindness. She admits she probably would have forgiven him for everything that happened during initiation. That Tris has the power to offer him forgiveness, even if that forgiveness is incomplete, makes her incredibly brave. She is almost completely at his mercy, and it wouldn't be out of character for Peter to respond to her kindness with more cruelty. But her admission prompts a shift in their relationship; it's more apparent on her end, but Peter's attitude toward Tris subtly changes as well.

Peter must have already planned to switch the serum so that she is just paralyzed instead of being killed, but on the way to her execution, he takes her past the window to Tobias' cell, allowing her one last look at him. He also offers her two words right before she is supposed to die: "Be brave" (*Insurgent*). These two words are significant in Dauntless and could have multiple meanings. Perhaps it's the way Peter says them that makes them kind. Something about them makes her think of Tobias and the fact that he told her the same thing before her first simulation. This makes her believe Peter is trying to ease her fear. These words are a clue that she isn't going to die, that she'll need to be brave for what's next. They're kind words said by someone from whom Tris has come to expect only cruelty. By saving her and then helping Tobias and Tris escape, Peter claims that this makes them even—that after she saved his life at Amity, he owed her, and now he doesn't anymore. Even though his reasons are selfish and warped, he is capable of kindness, and this is just the beginning of the change that we eventually see in Peter when he admits to not taking the memory inoculation because he's sick of being cruel.

Both Tris and Tobias claim to struggle with kindness more than any other virtue. Tobias tells Tris early on in *Divergent* that he doesn't want to put down the virtues of the other factions in order to be brave. He wants to be "brave and selfless, *and* smart, *and* kind, *and* honest" but he struggles with kindness the most. I don't believe he struggles with it as much as he thinks he does because I see so much evidence of his kindness throughout the series. Despite his plans to leave and become factionless, he stays in Dauntless to help Tris, and in *Allegiant*, he goes back to the city to tell Uriah's family what has happened to him. His efforts to stand up for others and to do what is right by them are often colored with kindness. The fact that he *believes* he struggles with kindness proves that he's thinking about it and that he values it. It doesn't surprise me that either he or Tris find the act of kindness is hard. They're forced to interact with people who are cruel on a daily basis, and it's exceptionally hard to be kind to people who have caused you pain in some way.

But that's what bravery is. It's not about hurting people or wishing pain on people who have hurt you. It's the realization that violence only begets more violence. It takes a truly brave person to break the cycle of cruelty and violence and use kindness in order to make peace.

THE NEED FOR TRUTH

It's not easy to look at Erudite and find an example of bravery, especially since Jeanine is Erudite's leader and it's the thirst for knowledge—to discover what Abnegation is hiding—that drives Caleb to betray Tris. During much of the series, the Erudite are cast as villains, but that's because, like Dauntless, they have strayed from the tenets of their faction, pursuing knowledge the way the Dauntless pursue a life free from fear. They've become arrogant, choosing to disregard the potential repercussions of their actions. This reckless pursuit of knowledge is what leads Jeanine to torture Tris, in order to develop a better understanding of her Divergence.

But the pursuit of knowledge can also be brave. When Tris and Tobias agree to go outside the compound in *Allegiant*, they are facing the unknown. Unlike during Dauntless initiation, neither of them is motivated by overcoming their innate fear of the unknown. This time is different—there's something out there, beyond the city limits, and though it's scary, they need to know what it is. There are countless dangers that could arise, but after seeing Edith Prior's video, Tris knows that they have a responsibility to do something with the truth about the city rather than just sit on the news as Evelyn wants. It's possible that what Tris learns about the world outside the fences will not be something she wants to know, but she knows she needs to seek the truth no matter the cost, and that is brave.

On a personal level, the knowledge she finds doesn't come without consequences. Tris learns exactly what it means to be "Divergent," which it turns out is a lot less special than she'd previously been led to believe. It's not the superpower she'd thought, and it's no longer armor that Tris can hide behind when she's afraid. She also learns that her mom knew David and knew about the Bureau and the experiments, and this knowledge about her mother, uncovering the secrets that she had, changes Tris' impression both of her mother and of her own identity.

It would have been easier, in many ways, for Tris to stay inside the walls, comfortable with her knowledge and understanding of the world. She still would have faced conflict inside the city, but she could have done that without having to change her perception of herself, her mother, or her world. She knows, though, that wouldn't be the brave choice. After escaping from her near-execution in *Insurgent*, she values her own life. She's realized that she wants to live, despite the guilt and the loss she's experienced, and with that realization, she wants to solve problems without violence and she wants to find the truth about who she is and about what happened to their society.

BEING HONEST ALL THE TIME

Similar to knowledge, honesty also costs something. Tris is good at holding on to her own secrets and not quite as good at trusting other people with the truth, something that often puts a strain on her relationships with the people she cares about, particularly Tobias. That's because it takes a certain kind of bravery to be honest and admit a truth that might influence how you're perceived by other people, especially those you care about.

When Tris and Tobias are arrested at Candor in *Insurgent* and given the truth serum, they both must admit secrets that they've kept from everyone else, including a few they've kept from each other. Tobias must admit the truth about the abuse he suffered at the hands of his father, that he chose Dauntless rather than Abnegation in order to get away from his father, and that the decision was actually born out of cowardice rather than bravery. Later, after beating his father to prove he isn't a coward, Tobias eventually begins to come to terms with this truth. By being forced to be honest with everyone, he can finally begin to be honest with himself about how his father's abuse has affected him. Although he initially intends to reset his mother's memories at the end of *Allegiant*, he chooses to confront her honestly instead, admitting that he betrayed her because he's as afraid of her as he was of his father. He risks a great deal of emotional pain if she chooses the factionless and her crusade over him. He knows she might not make the choice that he wants—that she doesn't want to hear that she is becoming like Marcus, the man who caused both of them so much pain—but he also holds out hope that they can reconcile and that he can reestablish his relationship with her. He's honest and he gives her a choice, and his bravery is rewarded when she chooses him.

As a true Divergent, Tris is in a different situation. She has the power to resist the truth serum, and she does. She struggles against it, trying to keep herself from telling everyone what happened to Will, but holding the information inside only intensifies the guilt that she feels for her actions. When asked about her regrets, she feels she can't hide anymore. She looks at Tobias and Christina and realizes she has to tell them the truth. She must admit that she shot Will during the attack on Abnegation. This admission is exceptionally hard for her, but not because she is feeling guilty and mourning Will's death. In fact, only by being honest and giving voice to what happened will she be able to move past her guilt and accept what she did. Instead, being honest about what happened is hard because, once the truth is out, Tris will feel bare. Everyone will be able to see Tris as she really is, not just as she wants them to see her, and she worries that her friends, especially Christina, will not be able to forgive her.

People are defined by their actions. Tobias has worked hard to appear strong and to keep the abuse he suffered at the hands of his father a secret so people will not think he is a coward, just as Tris has worked hard to prove not only to others but to herself that she is strong and brave, and to keep from focusing on the fact that she was willing to die for Tobias but never considered it when it came to Will. They both hold on to their secrets, wearing them like armor. Being honest and admitting these parts of themselves in front of people they know (and people they don't know) helps them be honest with themselves, confront their fears of rejection and inadequacy, and move on.

SELFLESSNESS AND BRAVERY AREN'T ALL THAT DIFFERENT

In the beginning of the series, Tris rejects her parents' values and beliefs. It's clear in the very beginning of *Divergent*, in the way Tris talks about Abnegation, that she doesn't believe in the ideals the faction represents. She finds selflessness stifling. Those feelings of rebellion are made tangible, and as a result more permanent, when she chooses to leave Abnegation and become Dauntless at the Choosing Ceremony. Once a member of Dauntless,

Tris tells Tobias that she feels selfish *and* brave, linking the two together. But she's wrong. Self*less*ness and bravery are entwined, something she gradually comes to understand over the course of the series.

For Tris, her mother's death in *Divergent* is the ultimate act of selfless bravery. Natalie Prior saves Tris from drowning, intending to get them both to safety and to join Tris' father and brother. However, when they are cornered by two groups of Dauntless, Natalie makes a split-second decision. She tells Tris to run and to meet up with her brother and father, and she tells her to be brave. Then she fires at the Dauntless in order to keep their focus on her, allowing Tris to escape. Natalie Prior knows that she is going to die. She knows that in order for Tris to escape she must sacrifice herself. But unlike Al's suicide earlier in the novel, Natalie's death is brave. She's calm and determined, and she sacrifices herself without expecting praise. She dies for Tris without hesitation because she loves her daughter no matter what and because she knows this is the only option that ensures Tris will live.

After her parents' deaths, Tris struggles with the concept of selflessness and sacrifice and what each means to her. She feels guilty for leaving her parents, and she wants to honor them by making their sacrifice for her mean something. She even wants to follow in their footsteps, essentially making them proud by sacrificing herself for the greater good. That's what drives her to turn herself in to Jeanine in *Insurgent* despite promising Tobias that she wouldn't. She thinks that she is being selfless, and in a way she is, but she's being reckless rather than brave. She's sacrificing herself because she can and because she feels guilty about her parents' deaths. Her sacrifice is not out of necessity. She had other options. She could have worked with Tobias and their allies in order to stop Jeanine rather than just resigning herself to death. Tris realizes this once she is facing her own execution and she's injected with what she thinks is a death serum. This is a crucial turning point for her character. She realizes that she values her own life and that she can be selfless and brave without sacrificing herself. She wants to honor her parents and their sacrifice by *living* and by helping people without violence.

By the end of *Allegiant*, Tris finally reconciles what it means to be both selfless and brave when Caleb volunteers to set off the memory serum in the Weapons Lab, even though he knows it will result in his death. He feels guilty about participating in Tris' torture, and as a result, he is willing to die so that she will finally forgive him. Because of everything she's been through, however, Tris knows that his sacrifice won't be brave; Caleb is making this choice out of guilt and shame. His sacrifice will be cowardly. He will surely die, because, unlike her, Caleb isn't Divergent and won't be able to resist the serum. Tris, though, has a chance. If she can resist the serum, there is a chance that she could do this and live. She knows that the plan itself is necessary—there are no other options. They need to get into the Weapons Lab. She also loves Caleb, despite everything he did and despite the fact that he hasn't been strong and brave. In fact, Tris is stronger and braver than her brother is, and that's why she makes the sacrifice for him. Because she now knows that true bravery is selfless, but it is also kind: "That self-sacrifice should be done from necessity, not without exhausting all other options. That it should be done for people who need your strength because they don't have enough of their own" (*Allegiant*).

BE BRAVE

Tris has always wanted to be brave—to prove to herself and to others that she is more than what she appears. The trials Tris went through in Dauntless initiation, things like standing still while knives spun toward her face and jumping off a roof, required her to act in spite of her fear. But it's the kind of bravery she exhibits in the small moments of her life that is more powerful. It's when Tris makes her decisions apart from faction loyalties, when she moves beyond the faction archetypes and is true to herself, that she's truly brave.

That is a huge part of her struggle throughout the series—coming to terms with her own identity. She never felt like she belonged in Abnegation, then she's tested and finds out that she is Divergent and doesn't really belong to any faction. Without being able to define herself by a faction or a value, Tris needs to learn to define herself on her own terms—not as Abnegation, or as Dauntless, or even as Divergent. She's more than Beatrice Prior, Tris, daughter of Andrew and Natalie, sister to Caleb, former Stiff, with six fears. She's more than the girl Tobias loves. All of these things are pieces of her identity, but they don't define her. By the time she reaches her death, at the end of *Allegiant*, she's found a way to honor all these parts of herself, these influences, while maintaining a distinct identity that is just *hers*. She's learned the same thing that Tobias is forced to recognize, when he must figure out how to move on without her—that "there are so many ways to be brave in this world" (*Allegiant*).

It's easy to see bravery in the big moments, whether in Divergent's world or our own. The fourteen-year-old who pulled two men out of the river before they drowned was brave. The high school baseball team who lifted a sedan in order to save a woman trapped inside was brave. The sixteen-year-old who went out on thin ice in order to pull another boy out of the freezing water was brave.

But there are ordinary acts of bravery all around us: a young man who enlists in the military after graduating high school because he believes in defending our country's freedoms, a young woman who leaves an abusive relationship, a girl in third grade who stands up for another girl when she's picked on by their classmates, a boy in seventh grade who tells the principal that a friend has brought a weapon to school, a transgender teen who tells his parents who he really is on the inside.

True bravery is doing the right thing even if you're afraid, being kind in the face of cruelty, pursuing knowledge no matter what you might find, being honest, putting others before yourself, and staying true to who you are.

Teenagers in our society sometimes end up with a bad rap. Adults think they're selfish and entitled or rude or even silly. I hear all the time from adults that young adult novels aren't realistic, not because of the paranormal or fantasy elements, but because a teenage girl wouldn't be able to save the world.

I think they're wrong. There are teenagers out there who are like Tris and Tobias. They might make mistakes, but they're intelligent and honest and kind and selfless.

They're brave.

Elizabeth Norris *briefly taught high school English and history before trading the Southern California beaches and sunshine for Manhattan's recent snowpocalyptic winter. She harbors dangerous addictions to guacamole, red velvet cupcakes, sushi, and Argo Tea, fortunately not all together. While she wishes she could honestly say she'd be Dauntless, she's probably not as tough as she thinks she is. She'd choose Erudite but manage not to be evil about it. Her novels,* Unraveling *and* Unbreakable, *are the story of one girl's fight to save her family, her world, and the one boy she never saw coming.*

We hear a lot about fear in Divergent. *It's the human weakness that Tris' chosen faction opposes, and much of the trilogy's first book is Tris learning about her response to fear and how to overcome it, or at least how to act in spite of it. For all we and Tris learn when it comes to controlling fear, however, we don't learn very much about fear itself: where it comes from, what makes overcoming it possible, and why doing so is easier for some people than for others. Blythe Woolston picks up that task here, bringing together one of* Divergent's *main preoccupations, fear, with one of* Allegiant's, *human biology.*

FEAR AND THE DAUNTLESS GIRL

BLYTHE WOOLSTON

This is a scare tactic. I will land safely at the bottom. That knowledge is the only thing that helps me step onto the ledge.
— *Divergent*

As Tris stands on the ledge over a gaping hole so deep and full of shadow it seems bottomless, she is confronted with some very potent triggers for fear: height, darkness, the unknown. Even more powerfully, she has witnessed another person, a girl like herself, fall and die. There is no doubt that death is only a tiny misstep away.

Tris experiences a healthy reaction to this real danger: her heart races, her muscles tense, her stomach lurches, and she gets goose bumps. Those symptoms of fear are familiar because we have all experienced them. Scientists call this the "fight-or-flight" response because these physiological changes make us ready to rumble—or run—for our lives.

But it doesn't take standing on the brink of an abyss to trigger those responses. A feather duster or pineapple can make a person freak out, freeze, and experience a full-blown state of fight or flight. What turns a pineapple into a source of terror? All you need to do is subtract light.

On a television reality show called *Total Blackout*, contestants blunder through pitch-dark rooms trying to accomplish a series of simple tasks like petting and identifying animals and inanimate objects. Meanwhile, the television audience gets to watch their struggles revealed via infrared photography. It is pretty funny to see a contestant terrified by the fuzzy pompom on top of a cozy winter hat. It would be a lot less funny to be that contestant, reaching out to touch the unknown, which could be a porcupine, scorpion, or the inside of a human mouth. What we can't see is scary. A multitude of little blue canary nightlights exist for that very reason.

Fear of the dark, and the unknown in it, is one of an assortment of fears shared by many people. Others include fear of swarms, fear of snakes, and fear of falling. These all appear in the fear landscapes and simulations featured in *Divergent*. Christina's wacky fear of moths? That's a swarm, and swarms are bad news. A single bee sting can make a horse flinch; thousands of bees can kill it. The snake tattooed behind Uriah's ear? Snakes probably writhe in his fear landscape, and if they do, he has a lot of company. Fear of snakes is not universal, but even people who aren't afraid of snakes can identify photos of them more quickly than other more mundane things.[1] Our ability to see and

---

[1] Association for Psychological Science. "Evolution of Aversion: Why Even Children Are Fearful of Snakes." *Science Daily*, 28 Feb. 2008. Accessed 11 Nov. 2013. <http://www.sciencedaily.com/releases/2008/02/080227121840.htm>.

to assess our surroundings is surprisingly skewed toward "snake detection." Research on macaque monkeys found far more vision-oriented brain cells dedicated to noticing snakes than anything else—even faces.[2] For good reason: snakes can be deadly. And Four's fear of heights? If you fall from the top of a ten-story tower, you might splatter like an egg on impact.

The connection between these common fears and real dangers is clear, but there are other fears that don't have such justification. Remember that scary feather duster in the dark room? A person suffering from alektorophobia, the fear of chickens, might be terrified by the sight of that duster in a well-lit room. The same person might find an egg horrifying. Unless you share that phobia, being afraid of an egg may seem ridiculous and incomprehensible.[3] It isn't a rational response. And that's part of the problem. Alektorophobia, like metrophobia (the fear of poetry) or the disorder nomophobia (the fear of being out of cell-phone contact), is completely irrational. Phobias are specific, persistent, intense fears that an individual *knows* are excessive or unreasonable. The alektrophobic understands that a live chicken can't "get" her, much less a feather duster or an egg, but that intellectual knowledge doesn't banish the emotion of fear. And that is really unfortunate because, while a chicken isn't a significant danger, *fear* of chickens can be a genuine threat to health and well-being. In fact, chronic fear, justified or not, causes stress, and stress causes everything from high

---

[2] Quan Van Le et al., "Pulvar Neurons Reveal Neurobiological Evidence of Past Selection for Rapid Detection of Snakes," *PNAS* (Oct. 28, 2013).

[3] I'm mildly alektorophobic myself. I had a bad experience with a flock of fowl when I was very small, and I never quite got over it. Imagine my fear landscape, where giant *chickens* roam—it's okay to laugh.

blood pressure and increased stroke risk to a greater vulnerability to cancer. There are a lot of people who wish they were Dauntless.

And that brings us back to Tris, standing frightened on the ledge—and acting despite that fear. How was she able to do that?

It wasn't because she was "fearless." The racing heart and goose bumps prove that. But something else is happening during those moments, and that something else is why she takes a step forward into the unknown: Tris is thinking. During those teeth-chattering seconds on the ledge, she analyzes the situation in a rational way. She weighs the evidence: the death she witnessed was an accident; the jump she is about to take is a test. When she bends her knees and jumps, it is a rational decision. Tris has taken one, two, three moments to process what she knows. And what she knows at that moment is that the fear she feels is all in her head. She is still experiencing the physical and emotional sensations of fear, but because she is able to reason, she can override those signals and choose to jump anyway.

If fear is "all in our heads," how does it get there?

Before we can answer that question, we need to understand what Tobias in *Allegiant* describes as "a complicated, mysterious piece of biological machinery"—the brain.

FEAR IS A GIFT FROM OUR ANCESTORS

Evolutionarily speaking, each of us is the conclusion of a success story. We exist because our ancestors lived at least long enough to reproduce before they drowned in a shipwreck, fell off a cliff, or were lunch for a cave bear. And fear played a role in that success. When it comes to survival, fear is a powerful advantage. It not only drives risk avoidance, it gives us our best shot at surviving when danger is unavoidable.

Charles Darwin, the sharp and observant mind that perceived the possibility of evolution, was very interested in fear. He conducted an experiment using himself as the subject. Here is his description of it:

> I put my face close to the thick glass-plate in front of a puff-adder in the Zoological Gardens, with the firm determination of not starting back if the snake struck at me; but, as soon as the blow was struck, my resolution went for nothing, and I jumped a yard or two backwards with astonishing rapidity. My will and reason were powerless against the imagination of a danger which had never been experienced.[4]

Why was Darwin so spooked?

It wasn't because he was a coward. Far from it. Darwin signed on for a voyage around the world aboard a wooden ship less than one hundred feet in length. *The Beagle* was the sort of ship known as a "coffin brig," notoriously hard to steer and prone to sinking. Darwin went because he wanted to collect scientific specimens, to slog through South American jungles crawling with snakes and spiders and critters with hungry bellies and sharp teeth. Field science is not a career for the squeamish. Then, after he returned, he published ideas that ran contrary to common belief and made him the target of harsh criticism. Every single one of those

---

[4] Darwin, Charles. *The Expression of the Emotions in Man and Animals.* New York: D. Appleton and Company, 1899.

decisions required courage. But when he visited the zoo, he couldn't control his body's reaction to the striking snake.

So what was going on? After repeated trials, Darwin was intellectually prepared for the puff adder's attack. His brain *knew* the glass barrier provided absolute protection. He wasn't surprised by the sudden appearance of the animal; he *knew* the snake would strike. But whenever it did, that certain knowledge evaporated and Darwin flinched. Fear got the better of him.

When it comes to understanding fear, we have an advantage that Darwin didn't. He could only observe the behavior of animals, including himself, and record the ways in which they all responded to danger or perceived threats. He could not see what was happening inside the bone box of the skull. Thanks to technology (fMRIs) we can actually watch a living brain at work. We can see which parts of the brain are active in response to pictures of spiders, snakes, and angry faces. We can, essentially, see fear happening inside our heads.

One thing that these studies have revealed is the outsized contribution to survival played by a little biological gizmo the size and shape of an almond called the amygdala.[5] It might not look like much, but when it comes to danger, it is the emergency first responder.

Remember the symptoms of fear that Tris experiences as she prepares to jump? They are all part of the wave of

---

[5] You actually have two amygdalae, one in each hemisphere of your brain. It's just easier to talk about one of them. In addition to the role it plays in fear, the amygdala is also involved in other emotions, memory, learning, and communication. Amygdala: tiny, but very influential.

responses the amygdala activates. It is the amygdala that prods the hypothalamus to release the cascade of chemicals and nerve impulses that jolt the entire system into fight-or-flight mode.

Her heart was "pounding so fast it hurts." That rapid heartbeat is a signal of changes through her circulatory system. Blood is flowing faster and more abundantly to the muscles in her arms and legs, the large muscles that are essential to running and defense. Her brain is also getting a richer supply of oxygen and energy through the bloodstream. Meanwhile, her arms are noticeably pale because the capillaries nearest her skin have contracted as part of the system-wide diversion of blood supply.

The "lurch" Tris feels in her stomach could be linked to a quick shutdown of her digestive system. As important as digestion is to survival in the long term, in the short term the energy required for that process can be put to better use elsewhere.

Even the goose bumps that rose on her arms are survival oriented. Granted, human goose bumps may not seem like much of a defense now, but once upon a time, our furrier ancestors might have benefited. Goose bumps are caused by the pilomotor reflex, which is the same reflex that makes a scared kitten puff up to three times its actual size. Appearing bigger can discourage potential enemies and might make the difference between being eaten for lunch and living to reproduce.

Why do all of these fear symptoms happen so fast? Neuroscientist Joseph LeDoux and his colleagues have been studying the role of the amygdala in fear responses and have discovered that certain kinds of sensory information—like sudden, loud noises—aren't processed and interpreted.

Instead, they are transmitted directly to the amygdala, jolting it into action. This fear circuit takes only milliseconds.[6] Since the information traveling on this shortcut isn't processed by the conscious part of our brains, the reactions aren't under conscious control; everything that happens, from changes in blood flow to the eruption of goose bumps, is involuntary.

Short of surgically removing the amygdala, there is no way to break this fear circuit. You can't "decide" not to respond because the reasoning, decision-making part of your brain isn't consulted. That's why Darwin couldn't stand still when the puff adder struck; he was being protected by a part of his brain that didn't take time to think things over. It was getting quick-and-dirty information—and acting immediately to keep him safe.

So, one important answer to the question about how fear gets into your head is this: you are born with it. Even newborns exhibit the fundamental fight-or-flight protective responses long before they can fight or flee. But there is another way that fear gets into our heads: we learn it.

FEAR IS A LEARNED RESPONSE, OR HOW TO TERRORIZE A BABY IN A FEW SIMPLE STEPS

Little Albert was about nine months old when he was used (and, it must be said, abused) as the subject of a psychological experiment done in 1920. If you have ever been around a little human at that age, you know they are curious creatures,

---

[6] During observation of a rat brain, the travel time was clocked at twelve milliseconds (.012 seconds).

interested in the world, and it can be a full-time job keeping them out of harm's way. This is how I imagine Little Albert to have been, and when I watch the movies made in the laboratory, when I see how interested he is in dogs, bunnies, white rats—even fire—I see a little brain learning all it can. Through his own experiential exploring (and hopefully with some parental protection), Little Albert would have learned that it's a bad idea to pet fire or to put his fingers in *that* part of the doggie. He would have learned about real dangers in the real world. But the researchers intervened and exposed him to a process that changed how he learned about fear.

While Little Albert was just looking around the room, thinking his little baby thoughts, the researchers banged on a metal pipe and made the sort of noise that causes the amygdala to go to red alert. Little Albert was—like you, me, or Charles Darwin—unable to control that fear response. Then the researchers started systematically linking that noise, and the fear response it evoked, to a little white rat. Before this "fear conditioning" Little Albert was interested in the rat. By the time he had been thoroughly "conditioned," he reacted to the sight of the rat with fear. It wasn't necessary to make the noise because his amygdala had learned to associate the animal with the horrific clang. It took no more than the sight of the rat to cause fear in Albert. Even worse, his little brain generalized his experience. At the end of the experiment, Little Albert was terrified of all furry things, even fur coats and Santa's white beard.

Sad as the story of Little Albert is (and it makes me want to cry), it did point the way to an important possibility regarding the control of fear. If fear can be learned through conditioning, it might also be possible to unlearn it. Through the process known as fear extinction, a fearful person is repeatedly exposed to a stimulus that causes fear. All of these encounters take place in a controlled situation where nothing bad happens. The person is encouraged to be aware that the fear they are experiencing is an overreaction. Eventually, the stimulus is "unlinked" from the fear response. Called counterconditioning, this system for unlearning fear essentially erodes the connection in the brain between a stimulus and a response. The technique is used therapeutically to assist those living with PTSD, chronic anxiety, and irrational phobias. While struggling with generalized anxiety, Veronica Roth herself found relief through counterconditioning that helped her retrain her brain. [7]

FEAR IS CONTAGIOUS, OR SEEING IS FEELING

There is at least one more way that fear gets into our heads: it's contagious. It doesn't spread by germs. We catch it via sight. When you see another experiencing fear, you are very likely to experience fear yourself. So fear can spread just fine without help from Jeanine's hallucinogens, fear serums, or transmitters. There are cells in your brain dedicated to making sure you catch fear from others. Those cells are called mirror neurons. As an Erudite scientist explains in *Insurgent*, "Mirror neurons fire both when one performs

---

[7] Ms. Roth sought therapy for her GAD years after she wrote *Divergent*. She shared her experience on this blog: Granger, John. "10 Questions with Veronica Roth, Author of the Divergent Trilogy, Part 3." *The Hogwarts Professor*. 6 March 2013. <http://www.hogwartsprofessor .com/10-questions-with-veronica-roth-author-of-the-divergent-trilogy -part-3-did-you-plan-these-books-no-really/>.

an action and when one sees another person performing that action. They allow us to imitate behavior."

Brain scans have caught this special category of cells at work and made it clear that they offer a wonderful advantage: they make it possible to learn that it is a bad idea to touch a hot stove without getting blistered fingers ourselves. Merely observing another's experience gives the brain the information that it needs to make the association between stimulus and response. That is a significant benefit in terms of survival.

Remember when Tris was on the brink of becoming the first initiate to master her fear and jump into the Dauntless headquarters? Mirror neurons—and Jeanine[8] says in *Insurgent* that Tris has an unusually high number of them—were active in her brain. Not only was her amygdala causing her to experience fear in response to direct sensory experience, the mirror neurons in her brain were registering the example of the poor, fallen girl.

But "catching fear" isn't the only function of mirror neurons. They are also essential to developing the social bonds that link us. The uncontrollable inclination to imitate others is called *modeling* by psychologists, and it is a shortcut to learning the ropes of social communication and co-operation. Mirror neurons don't just make us flinch when we see someone else stub a toe, they also make babies react to facial expressions by imitating them. Those shared facial expressions are the foundation of social bonds.

---

[8] According to Jeanine's logic, the abundance of mirror neurons in Tris' brain indicates that she is untrustworthy and a danger to others. Her mirror neurons make it easier for her to imitate others, to be deceptive, to be a spy. Unsurprisingly, Jeanine's is a distorted perspective.

Our mirror neurons may have originally evolved to help us avoid danger, but they have grown along with other aspects of our human brains, like the ability to think symbolically and use language. And when we hear a story, watch a play, or read a book, they make it possible for us to become emotionally invested in the lives of imaginary characters— like Tris, Tobias, and the other people we "know" through reading and observing in our imaginations while we read *Divergent*. It amazes me. When we read about Tris and her mirror neurons, mirror neurons are firing in our brains, too.

This is why we can become immersed in a story and why the characters in it become so real to us. This is why, according to recent research, reading fiction makes us more empathic. Reading stimulates the activation of mirror neurons, the same brain cells that are key to caring about others. If you were horrified and saddened by the treatment of Little Albert, if you cringe when a contestant on *Total Blackout* weeps and gropes in the darkness, if you cried at the end of Tris' story, you may have exhibited another capacity of the brain: the ability to experience the suffering of another. You experienced the power of mirror neurons to make us empathize.

Unfortunately, there is a limit to the power of mirror neurons, and it is related to their power to connect to those around us. Our mirror neurons fire more easily when we see a face like the faces we already know, which, in turn, makes it easier for us to communicate and cooperate, but what happens when we encounter a stranger, someone different from ourselves? In one telling experiment, researchers hooked subjects up to EEG monitors and showed them a series of videos of men picking up a glass of water. When the person in the video was of a different race or ethnicity from the subject, the subject's mirror neurons were less likely to activate.[9] Less activity can translate into less empathy, and reduced empathy can change the way we respond to others. When someone knocks on the door and requests help, activated mirror neurons can mean the difference between a helping hand and rejection. Without an empathic connection, all that remains is an unknown, and we have already discussed how terrifying the unknown can be.

It is easy to confuse difference with danger and be afraid. When that fear is coupled with a justification, no matter how flimsy, violence can result. Fight or flight? When it comes to encounters with other human beings, all too often, the choice is fight.

THE FUTURE CHICAGO EXPERIMENT, OR LOW-TECH, SLOW-FORM GENETIC ENGINEERING

When Tris escapes Chicago in *Allegiant*, she discovers that her Divergence isn't a flaw, it is the desired result of a generations-long experiment with the goal of "healing" genetic damage. The cause of that damage? The direct manipulation of genes. David refers to it as "editing humanity," but we call it genetic engineering.

Genetic engineering is the introduction or elimination of DNA in an organism. Say you want a plant that glows in the dark. You might try to take the firefly genes responsible

---

[9] Jennifer N. Gutsell and Michael Inzlicht, "Empathy Constrained: Prejudice Predicts Reduced Mental Simulation of Actions during Observation of Outgroups," *Journal of Experimental Social Psychology* (Sep. 2010).

for bioluminescence and introduce them into a plant's DNA. More usefully, if you want to study a human illness but need an animal model, you could use genetic engineering to create mice with a similar problem by inactivating key genes. These "knockout" mice are providing insight into cancer, heart disease, aging, and anxiety. Outside of the laboratory, genetic engineering is playing an increasing role in agriculture, creating crops that are more disease or drought resistant and even "immune" to herbicides. This is, of course, very controversial. Many worry about unforeseen consequences. And that brings us back to David and the origins of the future Chicago project.

Scientists in Divergent's world once tried to "knock out" the genes linked to negative traits like cowardice, dishonesty, and low intelligence. The results of that direct approach were catastrophic. On the individual level, eliminating a trait like cowardice resulted not only in courage, but in aggression and violence. Or as David explains to Tris, "Take away someone's aggression and you take away their motivation . . . Take away their selfishness and you take away their sense of self-preservation" (*Allegiant*). On the social level, the Purity Wars erupted.

Learning from this, the Bureau of Genetic Welfare decided to take a slower, less-invasive approach to genetic "improvement." They are willing to wait for generations to pass in order to eventually produce a higher number of "genetically healed humans." But slow approach or not, future Chicago is still another genetic experiment like the one that caused the Purity War to begin with. If we evaluate that experiment's design from a purely scientific point of view, it's a terrible plan, and unlikely to produce the desired results.

Basically, the future Chicago is a selective breeding

program. Selective breeding is a very ancient technology; humans have practiced it since the domestication of dogs and the dawn of agriculture. Every delicious pineapple, every fast-growing turkey with overdeveloped breast muscles, every potato destined to be french-fried is the result of generations of tinkering with genes via selective breeding.

Human beings are just as malleable as turkeys or pineapples. We are organisms that reproduce, passing along genetically coded traits. Some of those traits are easy to see, like eye color. Others are not so visible, like the inclination to take risks. Remember Darwin and his willingness to go sail off and slog through jungles? It is possible that he was influenced by his own "adventurer" gene. Even smoking cigarettes—that weird habit of the Candor—may be an expression of DNA. Research indicates that willingness to try the first cigarette is tied to a risk-taking gene, and addiction is also a genetic predisposition.

Nothing is simple when it comes to genes, and tinkering in hope of enhancing one trait can cause the emergence of another, unexpected trait, even when that tinkering isn't done directly to the DNA. A fifty-year-long fox-breeding experiment is great evidence of this. Russian geneticist Dmitry Belyaev focused his breeding program on a particular behavioral trait—tameness. Only the tamest members from each litter were allowed to mate. The resulting generations of foxes were tamer. They were very friendly and sociable around humans. But they also had floppier ears, a wider variety of coat colors, and shorter noses. If you selectively breed for tamer foxes, you end up with an animal that looks a lot like a domestic pooch. Judging by the products—like Jeanine and Eric—of the Bureau's long-term breeding program, future Chicago is full of unintended consequences.

What about the intended goal, the production of those desirable Divergents? Future Chicago is doomed to be less successful than the fox-breeding experiment for several reasons. First of all, there is no geneticist making the decisions about which of the subjects will mate and with whom. They keep track of the family trees, but they don't do what Belyaev did with the foxes by controlling which foxes mated. If the goal is Divergence, then a faction system that encourages mating from a limited gene pool where a single trait dominates is counterproductive. It's like trying to produce "tame" foxes by breeding from a closed-group selection of foxes that may or may not show any tendency to tameness. And all that is further complicated by the "Choosing Ceremony," where the breeding animals choose which gene pool to enter. (If the very idea of "captive breeding" of humans revolts you, it should. Ethical scientists would never behave in that way. But there is nothing ethical about science as practiced in the Divergent trilogy.)

Since the faction system makes the production of Divergence less efficient, why did the Bureau of Genetic Welfare build it into the social fabric of future Chicago? David tells Tris that this social order, with its clear cultural divisions, was meant to "incorporate a 'nurture' element."

Nurture matters, there is no doubt about that. A baby raised in an environment where sharing and generosity are valued is more likely to imitate those behaviors (go mirror neurons!). A baby raised in a culture where the rule is "spare the rod, spoil the child" is more likely to use violence to solve problems (mirror neurons, no!). The factions are designed to enhance the traits valued in each of those "cultures." And nurture doesn't only influence behavior. The effects of nurture (or the lack of it) can be inherited.

It's an amazing fact: if your grandmother or grandfather had a stressful life, you may be more prone to anxiety. The change isn't genetic; it is *epigenetic*. That prefix *epi-* means "on or above" and that's where your grandmother's hard life has left its traces—in proteins that encode on the outside of the chromosomes she passes down and that can affect the expression of certain genes. We know that environmental factors, like stress, can influence which genes get turned on and which ones don't. This may be one reason why stress can have such long-term effects on health: it actually can cause cells to grow abnormally and result in disease, even cancer. That is bad enough. That those stress-induced changes can move right along, borne by sperm and egg cells, into future generations is even worse.

There is new and dramatic evidence that fear itself can be inherited due to epigenetic transfer. Researcher Brian Dias conditioned a group of male mice to associate a specific smell with painful shocks.[10] (This is similar to the fear conditioning of Little Albert.) Later, those male mice fathered litters of pups, which shared their fathers' fear reaction to that scent without ever experiencing the pain. Those pups were born "knowing" what their fathers had learned the hard way. While the actual mechanics of this transference are still a mystery—this is far from settled science—it is clear that an environment rich in fear can have a remarkably lasting impact.

---

[10] Dias, B.G. and K.J. Ressler. "Presentation Abstract: 'Influencing behavior and neuroanatomy in the mammalian nervous system via ancestral experiences.'" Neuroscience 2013. 12 Nov. 2013. <http://www.abstract online.com/plan/ViewAbstract.aspx?mID=3236&sKey=b8777f87 -e87b-48ce-b047-9e2b36b833dc&cKey=b4c82dcd-2a7d-4393-b8bc -661cde6c2678&mKey=8d2a5bec-4825-4cd6-9439-b42bb151d1cf>.

So, while irreparably flawed as a system to create more "genetically healed" Divergents, the Chicago experiment does recognize the idea of nurture. However, the "nurturing" it provides is far from optimal. It may even be counterproductive, especially in Dauntless.

FEAR TAMING, DAUNTLESS STYLE

Let's apply what we know about the biology of fear to the Dauntless training program. Is it therapeutic? Does it provide the skills to control fear?

Let's start by considering Dauntless headquarters. It's a giant, dark hole in the ground that provides ample opportunities to die. What is the reasoning behind that? Tris sums it up pretty well when she says, "I have realized that part of being Dauntless is being willing to make things more difficult for yourself in order to be self-sufficient. There's nothing especially brave about wandering dark streets with no flashlight, but we are not supposed to need help, even from light" (*Divergent*). For Tris, negotiating Dauntless' dimly lit passages and rough floors is preparation for future moments when she will have nothing to depend on but herself. She imagines that to be a positive goal, but that sort of self-reliance comes at a cost. A culture that scorns "help" devalues teamwork and cooperation. The priorities of Dauntless are training and technology. Teamwork isn't on the list. And we learn from Tobias that both the faction's training and technology are becoming more brutal.

The simulations in the fear landscapes are a key part of Dauntless training. What happens during those sessions? As Tobias crisply describes the process to Jeanine in *Insurgent*, "The simulations stimulate the amygdala, which is responsible for processing fear, induce a hallucination based on that fear, and then transmit the data to a computer to be processed and observed." Knowing what we do about stimulating the amygdala, the cascade of fear responses, and counterconditioning, it seems possible that the simulations might be used therapeutically. Time spent in a personal fear landscape is an opportunity to confront specific stimuli in a controlled situation. It sounds very much like the program used in fear extinction. However, considering Four's repeated visits and the fact that his fears may change but are never extinguished, the technology doesn't seem to be any great advantage.

As advanced as Dauntless technology is in evoking fear, the techniques they use to tame it are simple. When Four prepares Tris for her first visit to her fear landscape in *Divergent*, he gives her this instruction: "Lower your heart rate and control your breathing." He might as well have said, "Deep, slow respirations cause a slowing of the pulse." That's how the principle was stated in a letter written in 1922.[11] It works, but it's not exactly cutting-edge technology in action.

As I was reading the Divergent trilogy, the multitude of serums made me curious: What about the potential for a "serum" that is an antidote to fear? Could we overcome fear with an injection?[12]

Research led by Moshe Szyf at McGill University indicates it is possible to "remove" the "residue" of fear from

---

[11] C. W. Lueders, "Voluntary Control of the Heart Rate through Respiration," *JAMA* 79 (1922).

[12] The fear of needles and injections is fairly common, but not in future Chicago, judging by the abundance of hypodermics and, in Dauntless, tattoos.

the brain. Ordinarily, rats neglected by their mothers are more fearful, less able to learn, and generally less healthy. But, when the researchers injected a drug called trichostatin A directly into the brains of rats deprived of nurturing care, that damage was undone.[13] The result has been compared to rebooting a computer. Knowing what we do about epigenetic harm, that "reboot" could even provide a long-term benefit, preventing the effects of stress from being inherited by future generations.

Another option might be a modification of the Bureau's memory serum. Instead of deleting memories as a means of social control, the memory serum might be better used to help individuals regain mental health. It appears to be an attainable goal. Researchers at The Scripps Research Institute have successfully targeted and erased specific memories from the brains of mice.[14] Eventually, it may be possible to alleviate the disruptive memories related to PTSD. We could even use it to help people overcome addictions by wiping out associated memories that trigger cravings. Those suffering from debilitating, irrational phobias might look forward to relief.

But there is another strategy that requires fewer needles in fewer brains. Instead of reversing the damage done by fear, it is possible to prevent it. A brain that grows up in a secure, nurturing environment is more resilient and more

---

[13] M. Szyf, I. Weaver, and M. Meaney, "Maternal Care, the Epigenome and Phenotypic Differences in Behavior," *Reproductive Toxicology* (2007).

[14] Erica J. Young et al., "Selective, Retrieval-Independent Disruption of Methamphetamine-Associated Memory by Actin Depolymerization," *Biological Psychiatry* (2013).

resistant to the negative effects of fear in the first place. Reliable kindness and love can serve as a sort of immunization. Maybe Tris is able to endure and persevere throughout her trials because she received a dose of emotional serum in the form of good nurturing that strengthened her and hastened her recovery from stress and trauma.

In terms of making people fear resistant, Dauntless training probably does more harm than good. It neglects fear "prevention" and focuses instead on overcoming physical reactions by repeated exposure, and we've already seen how damaging that sort of constant stress can be. But there is another, bigger problem regarding the culture of fear in Tris' Chicago, and it isn't limited to the Dauntless. The entire faction system is an incubator for a particular variety of fear: the fear of others (or otherness). And that fear is one that almost inevitably leads to violence.

FEAR AND VIOLENCE

Social systems that are inherently unjust breed insurrection. This dynamic echoes throughout the trilogy. Inside future Chicago, the factionless live in abject poverty doing menial jobs. Evelyn's "army" is composed of disenfranchised people without hope or opportunity. Outside, the world is divided into GP (genetically pure) and GD (genetically damaged). The GDs are lower status, which is brought home when Matthew tells Tobias the story of the violent attack on the girl he loved. The crime goes unpunished because the attackers are privileged GPs and the victim is considered to be less important. That injustice spurred Matthew to help Nita and her group of rebels. When the social order is so abusive, anarchy looks tempting. Tris observes in *Allegiant*: "It seems like the rebellions never stop . . . " The factionless, the Allegiant, and the GD rebels are all militant groups, and their militancy is always in reaction to a system that marginalizes them.

Honestly, the world of the Divergent trilogy looks a little too much like the one I live in now. When the Dauntless, under influence, take to the streets and massacre the Abnegation, the result is hard to distinguish from propaganda-fueled ethnic cleansings in Rwanda, Germany, and Armenia, where people were systematically targeted and killed because they were perceived as a threat.

It doesn't require hallucinations or activation of tiny transmitters to trigger that sort of violence. Remember the scene in *Allegiant* where the bullies attack a Candor boy because he has broken the dress code and is still wearing black and white? He wasn't wearing the right color clothes. I wish that scene was unbelievably exaggerated and not something that could ever happen, but in the real world people have been killed because they wore the wrong color bandana.

Gang violence, eugenics programs that focus on genetic "purity," and ethnic cleansing all have the same purpose: eradication of difference, the erasure of the Other. And the foundation of all of them is the same ancient fear. That same fear triggered the Purity War and flourishes in the fundamental distrust between the groups in future Chicago. It created a situation ripe for violence, and that violence occurred again and again.

We don't have to live mired in fear. We have alternatives. We can become more like Tris. We can think before we act. We can recognize the amygdala's response for what it is, an often-misguided overreaction. We can build on the empathic impulses born in our mirror neurons. We can learn to recognize our common humanity and respect difference.

We can be models not of fear, but of tolerance and compassion. We don't have to become the citizens of future Chicago; we could be free.

"Becoming fearless isn't the point. That's impossible. It's learning how to control your fear, and how to be free from it, that's the point."

—Tobias, *Divergent*

FEAR AND THE DAUNTLESS BOY

More than any other character in the book, Tobias is identified with and by his fears. He is called "Four" because he has only four fears. It is through his instruction of Tris and the other initiates that we learn how the fear landscapes work and what their role is in Dauntless training.

Let's take a walk though his fear landscape and look at each of his fears in light of what we know about how fear happens and why we fear the things we do.

We learn about his first fear, the fear of heights, even before his and Tris' visit to the simulation. When Tris climbs up the Ferris wheel during the capture-the-flag exercise, she guesses the truth when she sees how he behaves. When Tris asks about it, Four replies, "I ignore my fear." When presented with a height-related challenge in his fear landscape, Tobias leaps, demonstrating his ability to do just that. Stepping from the top of the Ferris wheel would have been a terrible plan, but in the simulated fear landscape, it's a smart move, since the goal is to ignore the fear, to neutralize it. Through his repeated visits to his fear landscape, it seems that Tobias has learned how to persevere despite his fear.

Confinement—claustrophobic confinement—is the second of the fears he confronts in his landscape. Claustrophobia is one of the many manifestations of the fear of smothering. Like the fear of heights, this fear is common enough to qualify as a "preset," but the fear in this case is compounded, made worse by his experiences as a child. His father used confinement in a closet as a punishment. That trauma amplifies the natural fear. One result is that this fear is more difficult to overcome. I have no idea how he usually solves this problem, but in this case, he is distracted and amused by Tris. It is only when he laughs out loud that this part of the trial ends.

Next is the situation where an armed woman presents a threat, but the apparent potential danger is not the fear at work. The challenge for Tobias is to pick up the gun and use it. He isn't in a panic, but he dreads this act. (What is the difference between dread and panic? Dread happens when there is time to think. It is what Tobias is forced to experience as he lifts the gun, loads the single bullet, and pulls the trigger.) In this scenario Tobias confronts his own capacity for violence. Killing the woman, coldly and methodically, is the only way forward. There is something both brutal and banal about this act, one Tris imagines him having committed within the fear landscape a thousand times before. She even observes that Tobias accomplishes this step without much difficulty, but she may be underestimating the toll this deliberate killing takes on him. The worst possible outcome, and the fear he faces here, may be the day this part of the scenario no longer elicits an emotional response like fear—when it no longer "feels real."

The next fear that he faces is his own father, Marcus, who abused Tobias repeatedly as a child. The scars of that sort of abuse run deeper than the marks left behind by the belt. Even now, when Tobias is an adult capable of fighting back, he cringes, defenseless against his abuser. The engine of the imagination has taken this traumatic memory and fused it with other fears: there are many Marcuses—a swarm of Marcuses—and the belts they carry slither like snakes.

As we learn in *Allegiant*, the fear landscape is always in flux. After Tobias faces and physically defeats Marcus in the real world, his fears change. Heights and smothering confinement still make an appearance, but he makes short work of them. That is when a new and horrible fear reveals itself. He is no longer afraid of suffering punishing abuse; he is afraid of the threat Marcus poses to his character, future, and identity. He is no longer afraid of Marcus the abuser, he is afraid of becoming that abuser. Tobias is afraid he will become like Marcus. It is a legitimate fear. One of the tragedies of child abuse is that those who experience or witness abuse are more likely to become abusers. This makes a certain sad sense when we think of the ways we learn as infants and children, of the mirror neurons in the brain, and how we imitate others. It is very difficult for Tobias to shake off that fear, to reclaim his own identity.

The final fear that Tobias faces is the fear of losing Tris.

When he leaves his fear landscape after he experiences the horrible grief of being unable to save her, he resolves not to use the simulation again. He doesn't need to relive his fears; he needs to overcome them in the real world. Because it is there, moment by moment, that he risks loving Tris. It is there, moment by moment, that Four becomes Tobias, no longer defined by his fears.

Blythe Woolston *would aspire to Erudite, fail catastrophically, and end up among the factionless. She is the author of* Black Helicopters, *a novel about a young suicide terrorist. Her earlier books,* The Freak Observer *and* Catch & Release, *reflect her interest in science. Her next book is full of imaginary monsters, because she needed a little vacation from the terrors of the real world, and wriggling tentacles are a pleasant change. She lives in Montana.*

If I had to sum up the Divergent trilogy in a single word (and, okay, if both choice *and* sacrifice *were taken), I'd pick* family. *Family and its attendant baggage are what drive most of Tris' and Tobias' decisions, whether we're talking Tris' commitment to protecting the information her parents died for or Tobias' fear of his father. Mary Borsellino delves further into the role of family, both in Tris' and Tobias' stories and in the series as a whole.*

THEY INJURE EACH OTHER IN THE SAME WAY

Family in the Divergent Trilogy

MARY BORSELLINO

The journey from childhood to adulthood is one that, by its very nature, requires us to leave behind the child versions of ourselves. This means that, in order to discover who we are and what our personal moral stances on the issues in our lives entails, we have to go through a process of rejecting our parents. It's normal, it's healthy, and it can be very frightening.

The Divergent novels tap into this fear, not only in the obvious ways, but also through the use of the archetypal Hero's Journey. In its most basic form, the hero's journey is this: a hero sets out on a quest to get something needed at home, accomplishes the quest and gets the prize, and then returns home with the prize in order to provide the help needed there. If you interpret the "prize" of the Divergent novels to be mature self-discovery, then it becomes clear that Tris is on this very same kind of journey throughout the series.

Because of the trilogy's structure, with each novel offering new layers of revelation about the true nature of society, it's not obvious at the outset of *Divergent* exactly what it is that is needed in the society—what it is that Tris must venture out and return with. Nevertheless, her story starts the way the hero's journey does: she leaves behind the family and life she's known. Over the course of the three books, she tries on different versions of herself, maturing and changing as life teaches her more lessons. Then, knowing herself and who she is, Tris returns "home" to the values that her parents taught her and leans on those values to find the strength and selflessness she needs to sacrifice herself for the future of those she cares about.

Even outside of the kind of life-and-death adventures found in fiction, this journey—rejecting your role as your parents' dependent child, discovering who you are apart from them, and then ultimately coming back to forge a new adult bond with them—is a huge part of what it means to grow up. As Tris and Tobias both discover, it's only once you know who you are outside of the context of your childhood family unit that you can come to know and understand your parents on equal footing.

It isn't until she's stopped living with her parents and being dependent on them that Tris learns anything about who Andrew and Natalie are as people, beyond their roles in her life as her father and mother. The further away Tris moves from childhood, the more complex her understanding of Natalie in particular becomes.

Adulthood is a role taken up at age sixteen in the faction system, when everyone has to choose which faction they belong in. For Tris, choosing to remain in Abnegation would still be a choice and would involve becoming an adult in the eyes of her parents—she imagines being able to talk to them at the dinner table, something she was never supposed to do as a child.

While none of us lives in a system quite like that of the five factions, there are rites of passage from childhood to adulthood in most societies, and some of them bear quite a strong resemblance to that of the Divergent novels. In Amish society, when teenagers turn sixteen they enter a period called *Rumspringa*. This is their opportunity to experience life outside the world they've grown up in, which like Tris' is one where pride is strongly discouraged and simple, community-centric lives are considered the best possible lifestyle. Amish teens on *Rumspringa* can try smoking, drinking, and hanging out with other kids their age.

Before they're sixteen, Amish children don't make any kind of oath to their church. Therefore, if they decide that life in the wider world is a much better fit for them—that they are more, say, Dauntless or Erudite than they are Abnegation—then their family ties remain intact. While it's pretty likely that parents of a teenager who leaves the Amish society feel dismayed by the choice their child has made, there's no culturally ingrained encouragement of rejection the way there is among the factions, of putting that choice of lifestyle above blood in importance.

Despite the comparatively lenient repercussions of choosing to leave, almost no Amish sixteen-year-olds go. The vast majority of them return to their families once they've had their taste of outside life, take their oaths to the church, and settle down. However, if they take the oath and then leave later on, they're shunned.

If *Rumspringa* is kinder than the Choosing Ceremony, shunning restores the balance by being much harsher. Shunning involves being forever an outsider. All family ties cease to exist: you no longer have a mother, or a father, or any siblings from your old life. If there's an equivalent to be found in the Divergent series, it's closer to being factionless than anything else.

Thinking about Veronica Roth's novels in terms of these Amish customs helps us understand that, in our real lives, changing factions and relinquishing any kind of family loyalty would be a huge step—one that would almost never be chosen by those offered it. If we look at the Choosing Ceremony as metaphorical, though, it broadens our ability to apply its lessons to our own lives.

It's quite common, especially in the United States, for young people to move away from home to live on campus when they start college. While homesickness and second-guessing are by no means rare emotions to go through, comparing this experience with that of faction transfers works best on a symbolic, heightened level. The fictional concept of the factions works as a barrier between our lives and the story, a filter through which we can explore ideas without having them cut too close to home. This heightened, more metaphorical kind of storytelling isn't universally employed in the novels on the subject of families—Tobias' family, in particular, gets a much more grounded and realistic treatment than many other facets of the books—but in Tris' story, it's used to great effect.

The dramatic, theatrical concept of the Choosing Ceremony gives outward shape to the very interior process that people of Tris and Tobias' age go through when they break away from the child-selves that were guided by their parents and begin to make choices on their own. By staging this developmentally necessary breaking away in such a grandiose way, with a ritual self-inflicted bloodletting in front of family and community instead of simply speaking or writing, Roth highlights just how difficult and emotionally complicated the process feels, however invisible it might be in most real lives.

In *Insurgent* and *Allegiant* we start to see the positive payoff that becoming an autonomous individual ultimately has for a person's relationship with their parents. Tragically, for Tris this positivity takes the shape of understanding who her parents *were*, rather than learning who they are, since her chance to have an adult bond with her parents is lost when they die violently.

Despite this, her journey of coming to love and accept them as separate individuals with personalities and histories of their own, rather than solely as her caregivers, remains. Only through the dissolution of the family unit they had before—daughter, son, father, mother—through Tris and Caleb's choosing factions for themselves can they ever even start to know each other as individual equals—Tris, Caleb, Andrew, Natalie. From the very first moments following Caleb's choice of Erudite, Tris begins to understand her family as having personal, private realities that don't necessarily match who she previously thought they were. This realization comes through especially strongly in *Divergent* with Natalie, even though Natalie interacts with Tris only a few brief times between Tris' Choosing Ceremony and Natalie's death. Even in those short interactions, Tris comes to see that her mother has facets and depths that Tris never began to imagine when their relationship was that of a dependent child and caregiving mother. That first dynamic had to reach its natural end as Tris grew up before the new iteration could take its place.

Tobias has a very different experience of family life than Tris. Though complicated and fraught at times, her relationship with her parents is fundamentally a healthy one—they protect her when she needs it most, helping her to escape execution and to infiltrate the Dauntless compound at the cost of their own lives. Though Caleb betrays her, he does so as her equal, after they've both become distinct adults. By contrast, Tobias is betrayed from a very early age by people whose moral obligation is to protect him.

Marcus is a violent bully and Evelyn makes the mistake of believing his violence is largely confined to his relationship with her—that Tobias will be spared the worst of it. Tobias, who is afraid of so little that his fearlessness is remarkable even among the Dauntless, is absolutely terrified of his father when he's young.

When Tobias publicly beats Marcus, an external observer might expect his childhood fear to be resolved by the act. But Tobias is far from a place of genuine emotional healing; striking and dominating Marcus instead morphs Tobias' fear from its childhood form into the more adult terror of becoming just like the man who frightened and abused him for so long. Tobias' awareness of his own fear of inheriting Marcus' darkness, and the self-control he deliberately exerts in order to actively avoid that path of development, suggests that it's not a likely outcome—but it's very easy to understand why Tobias is so frightened of it.

The depiction of familial abuse in the Divergent series is chillingly realistic—in a story otherwise dealing with the world through heightened sci-fi metaphors, the abuse Tobias suffers is shocking in its banal ugliness. He's scared of small spaces because he remembers being locked in them in his childhood. He knows he can't be Candor because of how many times he's lied to explain away the marks of his father's violence. He feels he is too broken from the abuse he's endured to ever belong in Amity.

Tris may not be used to demonstrative physical affection, but she doesn't flinch from it in automatic self-defense against an expected blow, as Tobias' instincts tell him to. The narrative of his own Choosing Ceremony, detailed in the short story *The Transfer*, breaks away from the first-step-to-adulthood pattern of the sixteen-year-olds the reader meets in *Divergent* and reads instead like the story of an abused youth running away from home.

Here, again, the concept of factions allows for a barrier between what the characters go through and what would be likely in a real-world equivalent of the situation. Fleeing as Tobias does would, in the real world, potentially entail conditions like those faced by the factionless—homelessness and poverty—rather than the opportunity that Tobias has of becoming a member of Dauntless. Natalie's flight from a violent home, told through her letters in *Allegiant*, is more in line with the reality of what someone in their midteens who has to get out, and get out now, might expect to face.

By the time *Allegiant* begins, the darker aspects of family bonds have been well and truly showcased: the violence between Tobias and Marcus, first in Tobias' childhood and then in his public retaliation; Tobias and Evelyn's brittle lack of trust in one another; and Caleb's betrayal of Tris. Which is why it's so remarkable that family becomes such a driving, positive force in the third novel. By demonstrating so many of the harder, more difficult aspects of what family can be, the series has paid the dues needed to then show that the immense, life-altering effect family can have on us is not necessarily one of pain but can also be one of great healing.

Sibling relationships play a complex role in the narrative of *Allegiant*, as families as a whole move to a more central place in the story. Tobias notes of Caleb and Tris' matching bruises—from when Tris lashed out violently in retaliation for the emotional hurt Caleb's betrayal caused her—that "this is what happens when siblings collide—they injure each other in the same way." But the mirror imaging that siblings in the novel display extends beyond bruises.

This mirroring isn't a brand-new idea when *Allegiant* begins—Cara has already stepped into the void left by her brother Will's death. But the theme becomes more pronounced in *Allegiant*, with Tori leaving the narrative and George almost immediately replacing her in the cast of adult Dauntless characters.

The Tori–George trade-off is especially worth talking about because it heavily foreshadows what will eventually occur when Tris takes Caleb's place on the final mission. Tori has long thought George dead, and it's as if her own death is the price the story demands before he can become part of the living cast. Tris is faced with the prospect of her own brother's death, but unlike Tori and George, there's no metaphor at play here. To rescue her brother from death, Tris must choose to die in his place.

The heart of *Allegiant*'s emotionally wrenching climax is made up of two themes, the first of which is sacrifice. Tris and Evelyn both relinquish something they have fought hard for—for Tris, life, and for Evelyn, power—in order to give someone in their family an opportunity to have a future. Caleb's future is a straight-up reprieve from death, and for

Tobias, it's the chance to begin healing from his traumatic childhood and build the beginnings of a relationship with Evelyn.

Soon after Tobias is reunited with his mother, he and Peter discuss Peter's decision to wipe his own memory rather than live with the decisions he's made. "You could just do the work, you know," Tobias tells him, and it's this same approach that lies ahead for Evelyn and her son. It's not a happy ending between them, but instead a promising beginning. A chance for the two of them to "do the work"—to build the first truly healthy parental relationship of Tobias' life, and give him a chance to heal from his monstrous childhood.

The second theme of the climax is motherly affirmation. After three novels and several side stories chronicling Tris' and Tobias' journeys through adolescence toward adulthood, the ultimate test for each of them involves coming face-to-face with his or her mother, and hope that these mothers will be proud, accepting, and affirming of the young adults they've become. This conclusion speaks to the real-world anxiety that readers have been facing and exploring throughout the series, confronting the fear that if they reject their childhood role within their families and begin to grow up, their parents won't welcome their new individuality with open arms.

For Tris, this last quest is back to the heart of the values instilled in her by her parents and her Abnegation upbringing. She had to first reject Abnegation in order to understand it properly and choose it for herself—to understand that sacrifice, rather than being a denial of her own importance and right to exist, instead could be an expression of deep love and protective feeling.

Throughout *Allegiant*, Natalie reappears as one of the cast of characters, but the reader now gets a chance to know a teenage Natalie, through her own words, rather than just as the enigmatic maternal figure she'd been before. As tough, defiant, and selfless as her daughter will later prove to be, the teenaged Natalie's journey into the adult mother present in *Divergent* offers a glimpse at the kind of adult Tobias might someday grow into: shaped, maybe scarred, by a traumatic childhood homelife and subsequent escape, but not irrevocably prevented from whole and compassionate adult life by the experience.

When Natalie speaks to Tris again as Tris dies, telling her, "My dear child, you've done so well," the "my" is a hugely important inclusion—Tris will always be *her* child, even now that Tris is no longer *a* child. Their reunion is not only that of a mother speaking to a daughter, but also that of a young woman dedicated to making life better for others speaking to the heir to her legacy. Through Tris' journey out of childhood and into her own identity, she's become her mother's equal when they finally meet again.

When Evelyn and Tobias meet in *Allegiant*'s climax, it's their deep, complicated emotional dynamic as mother and son, rather than any equal footing they have as individuals, that ultimately fuels their negotiations. Evelyn's internal processes and motivations are never given to the reader, but it's clear from her actions that her love for her son has long sat uncomfortably with her ambitions. Marcus has this internal schism as well but doesn't seem to suffer any crisis of conscience as a result of the clash between his domineering, aggressive nature and his duty of care to Tobias as a parent—he simply treats his family with the violence and cruelty his personality tends toward.

After three books' worth of bleakly realistic narrative about an abusive and emotionally neglectful household, Evelyn's choosing Tobias so absolutely over her hard-won power temporarily shifts their relationship from the literal to the symbolic, allowing their reunion to be the living mirror image of Tris and Natalie's afterlife embrace. But, in counterpoint to this heightened, thematic climax, the epilogue several years later gives us the more realistic version, offering us the chance to close the story both on the more symbolic level where so much of the Divergent series functions and also the grittier one where Tobias' story has played out.

Because the tone of the storytelling in *Divergent*, *Insurgent*, and *Allegiant*, along with the Tobias-centric side stories, can differ greatly depending on whether the subject in a given scene is science-fiction bioterrorism or a teenager trying to heal after escaping a violently abusive parent, it's almost surprising how coherently and consistently the themes of family rejection and then acceptance run through the story. Tris' arc, beginning as it does before her Choosing Ceremony, demonstrates how family plays a fundamental role in her emotional hero's journey. Tobias' struggle to work out what it means to be an adult, and to be Evelyn's child, when he has no blueprint to follow in playing those roles, is a different but equally important kind of heroism. As Tobias notes just before *Allegiant*'s epilogue, there are so many ways to be brave in this world.

At the end of the hero's journey, the hero returns home with the prize they've attained. In Tris' case, the return is ideological, as she comes to embrace the morality taught to her by her parents, even when faced with the ultimate test of resolve. For Tobias the return is physical, and he becomes a key part of the rebuilding of Chicago. He becomes a better version of his parents, working diligently in the field of politics to fairly attain power, rather than using the violence and manipulation his mother and father employed. Both Tris and Tobias learn to be the best person they can be from their parents, either by positive example or by surviving their failings. Thanks to their families, both Tris and Tobias discover what things in the world are worth dedicating their lives to, whatever form that sacrifice might take.

Mary Borsellino *is old-school Dauntless, the kind who gets her bruises stepping between bullies and the vulnerable. She certainly has enough tattoos to get along with the Dauntless, and visits Chicago often enough to know she's pretty fond of riding its trains! She writes dark fantasy YA novels and short stories of all kinds, loves writing Smart Pop essays, is a quiet but flamboyant extrovert and/or a noisy but thoughtful introvert, and works in the charitable sector in Melbourne, Australia.*

You could argue that the first two books of the Divergent trilogy are one big lie. Everything Tris knows—and therefore everything we know—about her world turns out to be wrong (or at least enormously deceptive). She and everyone she knows are living in a giant science experiment, constantly monitored and frequently manipulated to better suit the experimenters' goals.

The origins of Tris' city might be the biggest example of a lie revealed in the Divergent trilogy, but it's far from the only one. Debra Driza looks at secrets and lies in Tris' world, and whether Candor might not have had it right the whole time.

SECRETS AND LIES

DEBRA DRIZA

"The cruelest lies are often told in silence."
—Robert Louis Stevenson, *Virginibus Puerisque*

"Lies, lies, lies, yeah (they're gonna get you)"
—in the slightly less formal
words of the Thompson Twins

When I was a fledgling writer, still several years away from publication, I decided to get serious about this writing business. So, I did what any Super Serious Writer Type worth her weight in crumpled, tear-stained paper would do: I bought a magical storytelling pen. Okay, that's a lie—I mean, if I did have a magical storytelling pen, I certainly wouldn't be flaunting it to the entire world. Trust me, writers would KILL for that kind of precious.

No, the serious writer thing I did was join an online writer's forum. There, I was lucky enough to bond with other writers, both published and hoping-to-be-published; learn that stalking agents in bathrooms is frowned upon; and find critique partners. I struck up an early friendship with a young girl still in college, who was preparing to query agents with her novel. I remember my Extreme Awe at the snippets she'd post . . . snippets about a girl in a dystopian world where everything was divided into factions. When I was lucky enough to be among the first few to read an entire early draft, I knew. I just *knew*. This girl was going to get an agent, and then some.

And, WHOA. Did she EVER.

So, unlike my superlate introduction to both the Twilight craze (sparkle out!) and the Hunger Games phenomenon (okay, seriously, I love you, Suzanne Collins, but I can't lie—*Mockingjay* might make me a wee bit stabby!), I was a huge Divergent fan before the first book ever hit the stores. I've maintained an unabashed enthusiasm for Veronica's immense success all throughout her journey. (Wait—should I be calling her Ms. Roth? Or, once you serenade someone with Wham! hits, are last names a little silly?)

I imagine, at this point, my essay might seem a little digress-y (I do love a good digression. And bad dancing. Sometimes even to Wham!), but I did actually manage to squeeze two key words into the opening paragraph: lie and trust. Does that seem sneaky? Perhaps even a wee bit . . . *deceptive*? If so, what better way to start an essay on the Divergent series, which explores the nature of lying and deceit, and honesty and trust? The books caused me to think a great deal not only about who we lie to, why we do it, and how those lies affect relationships, but also about how governments use deceit to manipulate their citizens. At some point, I started wondering: Taken as a whole, what does the

Divergent series have to tell us about honesty and trust? Does the series suggest that ultimate truth is found within the Candor faction and their notion that lies destroy and the truth equals peace? Or does Ms. Roth's series (curses—I'm doing that weird, formal-name thing anyway!) suggest that lying is an acceptable manipulation—basically just another tool in a bag of survival tricks?

Looking at this another way—are honesty and the truth black and white, as the Candor see it? Or is the truth more like Fifty-plus Shades of Grey? (Oh, c'mon—you didn't really expect me to pass up an opportunity for a *Fifty Shades* joke, right?)

Actually, the way events play out in the series, I believe that lies and truth really are depicted in many shades of gray (just not, you know, shades of Christian Grey, because that's a TOTALLY different essay. Ahem. Moving on . . .). In fact, I'd argue that the best approach to truth and lies in the series, and in real life, mimics Candor's symbol: the unbalanced scales.

But before we explore that notion, let's look a little closer at how secrets, lies, and trust work in the context of the different relationships within the books.

DIRTY LITTLE SECRETS: GOVERNMENT, LEADERS, AND LIES, OH MY!

Oh, politicians. Whether we're talking present-day Rod Blagojevich auctioning off Senate seats while his wife works the reality television circuit, or *Divergent*'s futuristic, experimental Chicago, it seems like nothing ever changes in the Chicago political arena. There's always one thing you can count on: chances are, if politicians' lips are moving, they're probably not reciting a list of ways they've messed up. Or even the lyrics to "Thrift Shop" (though that would be super cool, wouldn't it?).

Though the various leaders in the Divergent trilogy are different in a number of ways, they all have one big drawback in common: they lie. To the extent that sometimes it seems as if they wouldn't know how to tell the truth even if they had a permanent IV drip of truth serum implanted in their respective, um . . . *arms.*

As with many dystopian novels, the leaders seek to control the masses. When it comes down to control in this series, faction (or lack thereof) seems to matter little, whether we're talking Jeanine from Erudite, Marcus from Abnegation, Evelyn with the factionless, or David at the Bureau. If there's one thing they can agree on, it's this: the key to controlling the masses is absolute power. And the tool each uses to obtain and retain that power is deception.

From the Erudite simulations that mind control the Divergent into killing the Abnegation in the first book, to Evelyn relieving her Dauntless allies of their weapons in *Insurgent*, to the multiple schemes the Bureau has going on in *Allegiant*, it's obvious that the power holders in this futuristic world have no qualms with fudging the facts. Actually, they're so good at hiding things we don't even find out who's running the show, or discover that Divergent-era Chicago is really just a giant petri dish over which the real folks in power hover with their magnifying glasses, "hmmming" and "ahhhing" as they see what transpires, until the final installment. Double crosses, machinations, plots and counterplots— Machiavelli would be rubbing his (supergrody, decomposing) hands together in this world, where those in charge behave as if the ends totally justify the means, and then some.

But maybe they use all those lies for good reason (well, if the good reason is "to keep people under their thumbs"). As Four ponders in *Allegiant*, "the truth changes everything." He agrees with Nita that by lying about the existence of war and violence prior to the genetic experimentation, the Bureau stole the people's right to decide for themselves what they believed about GDs. He concludes that "here, now, a lie has changed the struggle, a lie has shifted priorities forever." Finally, he realizes why it was so important to Tris to share Edith Prior's message: the truth is powerful. The truth can change the way people view the world around them and, in turn, change who and what they fight for.

Does the reason behind the constant manipulation really matter, though? Surely a morally sound government has an obligation to educate the citizens to the best of their ability and allow them to make informed decisions. To do otherwise is to treat them as something subhuman, or perhaps as toddlers, incapable of making rational decisions on their own. Even worse, when officials keep the masses underinformed in hopes of achieving a "greater good," it relieves the government of accountability and opens the door to corruption.

Can we really say, even in modern democratic countries, that the government never acts alone, secretively, supposedly to further the interests of its citizens? And if the citizens are kept in the dark, how can they ever trust that the government's decision making is both ethical and sound? One thing is for sure—the food for thought provided throughout the series on the ethics of leaders is quite a bit heartier than the Abnegation's dry bread.

In *Divergent*, the citizens are just pawns to maneuver

as the leaders see fit. And on the societal level, it's clear that lying isn't given a rousing endorsement by the main characters. If anything, lying and corruption in government seem to go together like Edward and Bella (only with much less sparkle).

WOULD I LIE TO YOU? SECRETS AND TRUTHS WITHIN RELATIONSHIPS

While it's obvious that Divergent makes a case for more truth in politics, what does the series have to say about truth in personal relationships? Does it make a case for the truth, the whole truth, and nothing but the truth? Well, that can be a little trickier to discern.

Family Ties—Matter of Trust

Lying by those in power is one thing; lying in the homestead another. Surely Tris can rely on those close to her to be up front with her?

Not so fast. In the dystopian chaos of the Divergent world, secrets are as much a staple in her Abnegation family relations as that dry bread (a big reason I never would have made it in that faction—butter is a glorious thing). By nature, the Abnegation faction seems to encourage lies of omission, since it's considered self-centered to talk about yourself. Secrets certainly aren't unfamiliar to those living in the Prior abode, whether it's Andrew Prior never mentioning the reason he hates Erudite so much is because he grew up there or Tris and Caleb never talking about feeling out of place in their parents' faction.

The biggest offender, though, has to be Natalie Prior.

In the first book, Tris discovers that her mom was a faction transfer—she was from Dauntless, not Abnegation. That's earth-shattering by itself. But then, in the third book, Tris gets a peek at a young Natalie Prior's diary, and everything she thinks she knows about her mom flies out the window. As it turns out, Natalie wasn't a faction native at all. Natalie came from the land beyond their city—from the fringe. Tris learns that her mom was inserted into the Chicago experiment in order to save the lives of Divergents.

Since Tris didn't know about these lies initially, that means they didn't affect her childhood, right? What she didn't know couldn't hurt her, and all that good stuff. Except this is the mother who helped shape Tris and her brother, Caleb, as they grew up in the Prior household. And there are a whole lot of psychologists who believe that when your loved ones lie, it affects intimacy. Those on the receiving end of the lies can clue in on a subconscious level and guard themselves accordingly. But the liars themselves can also be responsible for withholding intimacy, either consciously or subconsciously. Without trust, there can be no true intimacy, and the lying party is always aware that, because they are not telling, or cannot tell, the other person something, trust has been breached.

Does that idea have merit? Perhaps. Because when Caleb and Tris decide to defect from their native Abnegation, what's the first thing they do? Suck it up and tell their parents? Share their anxiety with their friends? Grab a box of Chips Ahoy! (wait, this is Abnegation—so more like a couple of dry chicken breasts) and hide together in sleeping bags in their bedroom while admitting their faction fears? Of course not, because in the Prior household, secret keeping is the norm. In the same tradition as their mom and dad, they tuck that information close to their chests, both of them too scared to admit the potential for massive family upheaval in their hearts. They act the same way their parents did, omitting the truth until the last possible second—at the Choosing Ceremony. (Sure, the test rules say you aren't supposed to share your results with anyone else—suggesting the faction system by its very nature encourages secrecy of a sort. But I can't imagine that's a rule everybody follows.)

And it's not like Tris' family is the lone set of Abnegation truth-tweakers. All you have to do to dispute that notion is to take a look at the secrets in Four's closet.

When you consider the family and faction dynamics, it's almost no wonder that Caleb withholds his decision to work with Jeanine at Erudite in *Insurgent*. This particular lie of omission leads to disastrous consequences both for his relationship with Tris and for Tris' safety.

Okay, fine, forget family . . . at least Tris can be honest with her friends. Right?

Why Can't We Be Friends?

When Tris joins Dauntless as a new initiate, it's a chance for a fresh start. Finally she can shed the weight of the Abnegation selflessness that has burdened her for so long! Finally she can be free and start forming completely honest relationships in a faction where it's not frowned upon as selfish to talk about yourself! Finally she can eat something with more flavor than an old shoe! Except—before Tris can even begin leaping from trains and learning to throw a mean knife, she's informed that she must keep a new secret. From everyone. As Tori informs her during her test, she's an oddity known as a Divergent, and she must keep that information hidden, at all costs—and for good reason. If Tris tells, her life might be in danger.

But surely that's okay, right? Surely this one little thing doesn't put an instant strain on her fledgling relationships?

Let's take a look.

Tris forms bonds with Christina, Will, and Al, but even at the beginning, we note that Christina, a former Candor member, is much more skilled in honesty than Tris. When Christina and Will kiss, what's the first thing Christina does? She tells Tris. But when Tris kisses Four, does Tris run out and tell Christina? Nope. And a relationship imbalance like that can be problematic. While it could be argued that Tris keeps that information secret because Four is an instructor, it's also pretty obvious that Christina would have divulged it if their situations were reversed. And it's not like Tris only holds the Divergent secret close, while in other areas she's an open book. Hardly. Multiple characters note that Tris is guarded and prickly. We see this time and time again, like when she doesn't tell anyone about her plan to sacrifice herself to the Erudite, or when she fails to confess to Christina that she was the one who shot Will.

Even Tris herself is aware of the burden her secret keeping places on her new relationships. She thinks in *Divergent*, "I should not lie to my friends. It creates barriers between us, and we already have more than I want." But perhaps even more telling is this quote: "I don't know when I accumulated so many secrets. Being Divergent. Fears. How I really feel about my friends, my family, Al, Tobias. Candor initiation would reach things that even the simulations can't touch; it would wreck me."

At least Tris is honest about her MO, which for much of the first books, seems to go something like this: *when in doubt about someone's reaction to the truth, hide it.* Even though her innate distrustfulness isn't doing her relationships any favors.

Tell Me Sweet Little Lies—Fudging the Truth with Significant Others

At first, it appears that the one person who might break through Tris' trust issue is Four. I don't think it's a coincidence that in *Divergent*, Four is both a) one of two people who know the truth about her and b) the person she becomes the closest to, and vice versa. Okay, so sure, the fact that Four is ethical (in a crowd of the morally challenged), strong, and more than just a little hot probably has a teensy bit to do with Tris' attraction. But is it just a coincidence that Four is also the only one who knows her Divergent status? Since Four has already discovered her closely guarded secret, Tris doesn't have to hold back with him, which undoubtedly fosters a unique sense of intimacy between them. In sharing that secret, they create a bond. He knows the real her. Not only that, he shares his own deep, dark secret, letting her in to see the real him—the young boy, frightened of an abusive father. Tris is the only one, outside of Four and his parents, who knows about the abuse he and his mom withstood at the hands of his politician father, and he shows her in one of the most personal ways ever—via insertion into his private fear landscape. Talk about trust.

In this sense, we are presented with a strong case for the argument that the truth can bind us to others. In other instances, Tris shows us that lies can wedge us apart.

For example, when Tris doesn't tell Four that she killed Will, he senses something is amiss. He even asks her outright if something is wrong and if she still trusts him. Though the weight of keeping secrets feels terrible—"maybe time would not feel as heavy if I didn't have this guilt—the guilt of knowing the truth and stuffing it down where no one can see it"—she lies yet again. By the time Four discovers the truth during the truth serum confession, he feels understandably betrayed. But maybe it's easier for her to remain guarded, since she knows Four is holding things back from her, too. Big things, as it turns out—that his mom is still alive and that he's been considering allying with Evelyn and the factionless. Perhaps the real lesson here is that the trust that comes from honesty starts out as a two-way street, but when one lane shuts down, the other does as well.

Luckily, the same principle works in reverse: when Tris and Four start being more honest with each other again, their relationship grows. In *Allegiant*, Nita tries to persuade Four to keep Tris in the dark about their meetings by telling him the information would put her in danger. But Four is far too aware that their recently restored trust is fragile and that in order to preserve their relationship, he must tell the truth. Though they still have their ups and downs after this point, Tris and Four are finally able to trust each other enough to be fully open and vulnerable, and that leads to them consummating their love via physical intimacy (or as we in the YA world like to say: sexy times).

SELF-DECEPTION IN DIVERGENT-LAND—AN ACCEPTABLE SUBTERFUGE IN A HARSH WORLD?

We've talked about lying and deceit in regard to multiple relationships throughout the Divergent series—on the part of leaders, among family, between friends and would-be lovers. But what about your most intimate relationship? What happens when you lie to yourself?

Nothing good, that's for sure. If there is one truth to be had in the Divergent series, I believe it's this: that you can lie to your friends, and you can lie to your nose, but you can't ever . . . wait. Strike that. You can totally lie to your friends' noses. Actually, it's this: that lying to yourself is never okay, and that ultimately, the person it's most important to always be truthful with is yourself. When you try to hide or subvert your true feelings or nature, things can go horribly, terribly wrong. When Tris refuses to acknowledge the depth of her despair over her role in Will's death, for example, that little self-deception almost gets her killed.

Ironically, as tear-jerking and Kleenex-grabbing a thing as self-truth is, I believe this is the key to understanding the importance of Tris' ultimate sacrifice in *Allegiant*. She has to search deep inside to realize not just the truth behind her brother's actions—that he's sacrificing himself out of guilt, not love—but also the truth that beats in her own heart about what she can live with, and what's worth dying for.

The only character who really avoids his own truth is Peter, and that's only through resetting his memories entirely—a very drastic step. (Okay, the folks at the Bureau did, too, but they didn't exactly wrestle Four to the ground for the chance. Involuntary avoidance doesn't count.) People can attempt to disregard the reality of who they are, but deep down, they just can't ignore it. Just like when Tris tries to pretend that it's okay for Caleb to sacrifice himself for the wrong reasons—she can hide from the truth for only so long. Ultimately, she realizes that if she allows Caleb to die because of guilt versus love, she will never be able to live with herself. She would rather die being true to her beliefs than live suppressing them. She'd rather accept her values and go down fighting for them. By the end of the Divergent trilogy, it appears that self-realization and honesty trump all.

Hold up, though. We've seen how lying and deception abound in the Divergent-verse, even at the hands of our heroine, Tris. Does that mean that, gasp!, Candor was the way to go, all along? Was Ms. Roth pulling a fast one on us? Should we all tattoo the Candor manifesto on our bodies and read it to each other every night before bed?

CANDOR: BRUTAL HONESTY FOR THE WIN, OR JUST PLAIN MEAN?

The Candor faction was formed by people who blamed all the world's problems on deception and dishonesty. They believe the root of war lies in duplicity. They even say, point-blank in their manifesto, that "Dishonesty makes evil possible."

Does that hold up to scrutiny within the pages of the books? On a macrolevel, yes. In terms of government and big lies, Candor might just be on to something. The biggest evil in the book seems to center around the corruption of power, and that corruption is without fail linked to duplicity. But does that mean that Candor is always right, even in regard to smaller-scale interactions? Because the Candor have a lot to say there, as well.

Candor is the faction responsible for such gems as "politeness is deception in pretty packaging" and "lying to spare a person's feelings, even when the truth would help them to improve, damages them in the long run."

That latter sentiment might sound noble in theory, but who gets to decide which truths help people improve? Isn't it possible that some truths are just hurtful?

What Candor is basically saying is that the greatest moral good is honesty. That truthfulness is more crucial than anything else—even causing others pain. Does the series support this claim? Not so much.

Candor might be honest, but they're also often seen as cruel. There's a reason their workplace is dubbed the "Merciless Mart." A reason they're always bickering. A reason people in their faction are seen as a little abrasive.

Plus, their motto that "honesty leads to peace"? That sounds a wee bit oversimplified. So, if the Bureau had just fessed up to the folks in Chicago that they were the lucky participants in a massive experiment in Faulty Genes, everything would have been a-okay? Doubtful.

What is the series' final position on lying, then?

By the end of *Allegiant*, I think a clear case has been made that lying is not the worst sin you can commit in Divergent-land. There are too many instances when lying is supported by positive outcomes. Granted, this type of dishonesty in the book usually only comes guilt-free when employed in life-and-death scenarios, like when Peter lies to save Tris from Jeanine, or when Tris lies under the truth serum to save Cara and Christina from being labeled as traitors, or when Tris lies to David to save the people in Chicago. If dishonesty and deception were being depicted as the scourge of all mankind, then Candor would have ruled the day at the conclusion, case closed.

Of course, the converse—keeping the peace at all costs, even if it means lying—is not shown in a necessarily flattering light, either. Amity's ease at lying isn't really portrayed as the be-all and end-all of faction manifestos, either.

Instead, the truth lies somewhere in the middle, and different factors necessarily weigh into decisions to lie or not to lie. Self-serving lies are possibly shown to be the most damaging—like those of the leaders to the citizens, or when Tris lies about shooting Will. But lies to protect yourself or others from danger? There we are, back in that gray zone. There's no easy answer, which makes this dilemma a more compelling one for discussion. I don't think the books suggest that lying is always the worst thing you can do and telling the truth is always the best—or vice versa.

Ultimately, I think the trilogy makes a case that sparing others unnecessary pain can tip the scales in favor of lying. But the scales are just that—*tipped*. While Candor's manifesto might not be the ultimate truth, their symbol proves to be far more on the mark: unbalanced scales, always in motion, always weighing the virtue of truth against the necessity of lies.

In the end, it appears that lying and honesty are both a ratios game. Or perhaps a balancing act. Maybe every deed is weighed, like on that Candor scale. When little lies are small and innocuous—like, "yes, your butt looks good in those jeans"—they amount to the mass of a flea. Whereas the big, painful whoppers are more comparable to an elephant. But even the big lies appear to be lightened by intent. Did the person lie for selfish reasons? Or to spare others pain? I think that the actions and consequences we see in the series persuade us that all of these things matter, that lying to spare others doesn't necessarily mean ruining relationships, so long as the balance remains tipped toward the truth—and as long as, in the end, the one person you never lie to is yourself.

What it all boils down to is this: maybe I was on to something with this whole Fifty-plus Shades of Grey thing. In fact, I can imagine the Fifty Shades of Divergent spin-off now.

Sorry, Veronica . . . but if I'm being totally honest, the idea of Four in a tie is just too much to resist.

Debra Driza *is a former physical therapist who much prefers torturing fictional characters over live humans. She's particularly fond of sweets, adding random colors to her hair, Rhodesian Ridgebacks, and teen TV. Please don't ask her to locate anything in her purse, aka "the black hole of doom." While she likes to think she's Dauntless sometimes, she's pretty sure the faction members would chuck her into the chasm over her impromptu singing and dancing. MILA 2.0 is her first novel, and the first in a YA sci-fi thriller trilogy from HarperCollins.*

Factions are a fact of life in the Divergent trilogy, and I'm not just talking about the five Tris details at the story's start. The word faction, *as used in our world, could technically describe the group of Dauntless loyal to Jeanine, or even the factionless, united as they are under Evelyn's leadership and against the faction system.*

So it should be no surprise that, almost immediately after learning about the Bureau of Genetic Welfare, we are introduced to another, opposing faction: the GD rebels. And as with Jeanine and Evelyn, neither side turns out to be especially honorable. Faced with a choice between less than ideal options, how do you decide? Dan Krokos has a few ideas.

BUREAU VERSUS REBELS:
WHICH IS WORSE?

DAN KROKOS

Warning: Below you will find many spoilers about *Allegiant*. Turn back now if you haven't read it. Are you still here? Are you sure. Let us be Erudite-sure before moving forward.

Okay. Now that those losers are gone, I'd like your help in deciding something. In *Allegiant*, we are introduced to two "factions" outside the city limits. In one corner is the Bureau of Genetic Welfare, a government agency that has been around for at least seven generations. Its purpose: to rid the world of genetic damage once and for all. In the opposing corner: the rebels, a group of genetically damaged (GD) individuals who live in the sparsely populated "fringe" areas between cities.

Both sides are terrible, responsible for death and

destruction inside and outside of Chicago. Both operate in a way that results in the deaths of innocent people.

But which side is worse?

In our world, we're forced to choose between the lesser of two evils every day, and the world of Divergent is no different. Tris makes her choice in the end, aligning herself with the rebels' cause.

But was she right?

A BRIEF DIGRESSION ABOUT OTHER TERRIBLE PEOPLE

I thought about including Evelyn and the factionless in this debate, as they make up what feels like the third major player in *Allegiant*, having an even larger role than the Allegiant themselves, it seems, but the *why* of their struggle is much less interesting to me. Evelyn, while clearly sincere in her quest to end the faction system, mostly wants to control everything. In this, she's much more like the major players earlier in the trilogy than like the Bureau and the rebels. Marcus Eaton and Jeanine Matthews also just want to control everything (although functionally Jeanine's more like a mad dog given the tools for chaos, not so different from the Joker). None of these power-hungry maniacs are as cool as the two sides who feel deep down they're on the right side of things.

I knew Evelyn couldn't really be someone I took seriously when she said, "The factions are evil. They cannot be restored. I would sooner see us all destroyed" (*Allegiant*). Thank you, Evelyn, for opening your bag of marbles and showing us you have none. Someone should tell her that in her quest to destroy the factions, she nearly became the two people she hates most.

IN THIS CORNER: THE BUREAU

When the Bureau is first introduced, it's after Tris and friends finally leave the city that has caused them so much pain but has, at the same time, been the only thing they've ever known. Literally. Like, they don't know what airplanes are. Or that their city was called Chicago once upon a time, just a few centuries back. While that sounds nuts, I kind of envy their ignorance and the simple life their isolation led to. The city clearly held thousands of people, but through the factions, I think it was possible for most of them to find a fulfilling place in the world that they knew. (And I do mean *world*; many characters in *Allegiant* are startled to find out just how big the world outside the fence really is.)

There's a reason the Allegiant are ready to fight against Evelyn to preserve their way of life—it worked. Maybe not as well as it could have, but *Divergent*'s Chicago was a self-sustaining community that enjoyed long stretches of peace, probably much longer than the ones we experience out here in the real world.

Then David, the Metamucil-y leader of the Bureau of Genetic Welfare, has to ruin everything. He tells Tris and friends the truth: the city is an experiment. The goal? To cure genetic damage.

Tris and friends naturally don't like the idea that they've been human guinea pigs, or that almost everyone they know is genetically damaged (including many of them)—who would? Christina makes a wonderful point when Tris asks her what she thinks about the idea of being genetically damaged: "No one likes to be told there's something wrong with them, especially something like their genes, which they can't change." Too true.

But David talks about the experiment like it's a good thing, and he has proof. Chicago is not the only experiment. Other cities, like Indianapolis, didn't have the faction structure (based on the five varieties of genetic defects) that Chicago has. And the result? Complete destruction within three generations.

It must be jarring to learn your community isn't really real, but think about this—before Jeanine decided to be the second coming of Genghis Khan, life in Chicago wasn't all that bad. Yeah, being factionless was a real bummer, but the majority of people—thousands and thousands—enjoyed life in their factions. They had food and fellowship and shelter: all the key ingredients for happiness. If the Bureau hadn't put them there, they'd be on the street in the outside world, scraping by with the other people in the fringe, living hour by hour in search of food.

When Tris and friends arrive at the Bureau, David spells out exactly what genetic damage is: "Take away someone's fear, or low intelligence, or dishonesty . . . and you take away their compassion. Take away someone's aggression and you take away their motivation, or their ability to assert themselves. Take away their selfishness and you take away their sense of self-preservation."

As David explains, a few hundred years ago the government attempted to "fix" certain people by tampering with their genes, trying to take away their fear, stupidity, dishonesty, aggression, or selfishness. They didn't know what the ramifications would be, and it resulted in the greatest disaster ever manufactured by humans.

Genetic damage is not an opinion; you can see it at work in the factions. If the damage was just a made-up thing, everyone would be Divergent. Kids would grow up in Abnegation and be like, "Why the EFF can't I look at myself in the mirror?" as Tris is almost scolded for doing on page one of the series. A Candor man might suddenly want to add a few shades to his wardrobe, or to stop blurting out the "truth" like some kind of insane person.

(Only the Amity faction seems to have nothing wrong with them. "Peaceful but passive," Tris describes them in *Allegiant*. There are worse things to be than a bunch of hippies who want to dance around in their orchards and smile at each other.)

Now imagine people like this mixed in with the general population, with no faction to make them feel like they're a part of something. No real explanation for why they feel the way they do. They are not less or more than human, not one bit, but you can see how their differences would give rise to conflict. Also known as the Purity War.

Here is where I think David is full of crap. He describes the Purity War as "a civil war, waged by those with damaged genes, against the government and everyone with pure genes." As if. David, we know what happens in America when citizens are confronted with people unlike them. The year is 2014, and we still won't allow certain people to marry each other, simply because some other people *don't like it*. That's it.

I'm sure the GDs, especially the volatile ones like the Candor-types and Dauntless-types, were capable of aggression, but the Bureau's claiming the conflict was one-sided should've been a red flag for Tris and friends right from the start. Think about it: (almost) every conflict can be traced back to one group not liking what another group is doing, or wanting whatever that group has. We didn't like communism in Vietnam. The British didn't like that we weren't paying enough taxes. Iron Man doesn't like that Captain America is kind of an officious douchebag.

Conditions in America had to have been pretty bad for the war to start in the first place, considering there is no outward way to tell if someone is genetically damaged. We know the government didn't keep a record, since GDs were asked to come forward when the experiments first started. So maybe the city experiments aren't such a terrible thing after all.

Furthermore, where is the proof that the Bureau is actively oppressing people in the outside world? It sounds like they have their hands full with the experiments inside Chicago and across the Midwest. When they do venture into the fringe areas and go on raids, they don't kill people. Instead, they pull children from the gutters and deliver them to orphanages (though we don't know if these children are GPs, or GDs, and what ultimately happens to them; it's hard to count this as a pro without more details).

It's no secret the fringe is a lawless wasteland. Sure, when Tobias visits the fringe, a guard explains why some people choose fringe life: "Here, there's a chance that if you die, someone will care." That's not really comforting. Yes, the GDs inside Chicago were watched. Yes, they were controlled by the careful application of various serums. But I'd take that over living in ruins, waiting for someone to slip a knife under my jaw to steal whatever meager belongings I had acquired.

On the flip side, the Bureau is all about reinforcing ideas that lead to societal oppression. They oppress in subtler ways than turning fire hoses on people: Nita, for example, is extremely intelligent and obviously capable, yet she isn't allowed to progress beyond her station. The fringe *exists* because of the Bureau. If tomorrow someone proved that genetic damage doesn't necessarily have a huge impact on a person's actions, the Bureau's purpose—and society as everyone knows it, divided between GD and GP—would be dust. It's hard to trust an institution whose very existence depends on the idea they're in charge of verifying.

If only the Bureau had been able to evolve, to maintain the ideals of their cause without stooping to murder. If you're trying to make the world a better place, it's hard to be credible with blood on your hands. All the Bureau ends up illustrating is that genetically pure people are capable of immense destruction and oppression, too.

At least with a GD, you can estimate in what way they may or may not be destructive. The Choosing Ceremony only confirms this—you really have to be predisposed to switch from the faction you've been raised in to another faction where you don't know anyone. You'd have to truly believe you belong somewhere else.

Tobias, for instance, says he has a great capacity for cruelty; he is aggressive and enjoys hurting others. We don't know exactly *how* Tobias is damaged, so it could be argued that he learned how to be cruel from his father, Marcus (a man who is supposed to be genetically pure, by the way). It would not be insane to argue that a boy grows up to be like the man who raised him. Either way, Abnegation—home of the selfless, those with no sense of self-preservation—is no place for him. It probably wouldn't have been a place for him even if he hadn't been trying to escape his father. And think of people like Peter, who fit the Dauntless model for aggression even more (and possess the defect the Dauntless are known for—lacking compassion).

If we can agree that the factions are *not* pulled from

thin air, and really do help GDs live in harmony—and as I stated earlier, Indianapolis and other failed cities are proof of this—then a GD in a faction system may be less dangerous overall.

GDs are predictable. Meanwhile, who knows what a GP will do?

IN THE OTHER CORNER: THE REBELS

Now let's look at Juanita and her band of merry rebels. Right away they get bonus points just for fighting against oppression, an oppression that perhaps GPs, in their sense of superiority, are too blind to see. But is that enough to forgive their tactics?

Fighting the good fight only goes so far when your means to an end are downright evil. We already know Nita is a practiced liar, having worked her way up the Bureau's ladder, but she's also adept at subtler manipulation. Part of the power behind the rebellion sales pitch she gives Tobias is from the Bureau's—and David's—lack of specificity about Tobias' genetic damage. When Tobias' genes are tested, he is not told how they are damaged, or what it means, or how/if it affects who he is as a human being. He's simply told that he's damaged, that he's prone to mess up. Of course he'd be more susceptible to Juanita's offer. She knows just how to come at him, too. Her opening line, when she thinks he's just vulnerable enough to be taken in: "See, I'm not really on board with being classified as 'damaged.'"

Nita doesn't even offer up any real proof the Bureau is bad—not at first. "I can show you evidence," she says, "but that will have to come later." Yet Tobias is still willing to go along with the rebels' plan, resulting in the death of his friend Uriah and almost causing him to lose Tris, which is the only thing he really seems to care about.

Later, Nita shows Tris and Tobias that the Bureau supplied the serum used to control the Dauntless at the end of *Divergent*, the serum indirectly responsible for the death of Tris' parents. That's why I understand Tris immediately wanting nothing to do with the Bureau. Providing Jeanine with that serum is truly an unforgiveable act. But so is setting off explosives inside the Bureau, killing innocent people—namely Uriah, the only guy who was able to maintain a smile through all three books.

Though Nita hates what the Bureau has done to the Abnegation, she can't really argue that trying to prevent the collapse of the faction system wasn't for the greater good. The current state of the city in *Allegiant* is proof of that. Nita's words: "Evelyn is effectively a dictator, the factionless are squashing the faction members . . . Many people will die."

Nita's argument against the Bureau really crumbles when she tells Tobias, "If we believe we're not 'damaged,' then we're saying that everything they're doing—the experiments, the genetic alterations, all of it—is a waste of time."

A person can't believe they're genetically damaged or not. The science is there. And by using deadly force, Juanita and the rebels are reinforcing the deeply held (though extremely bigoted) belief that genetically damaged individuals are inferior—crude humans prone to violence who caused a war that almost resulted in the destruction of everyone in America. Imagine if instead the rebels led by example and organized some kind of society on their own where GDs had a role, where peace was kept, and where they could show the Bureau that being GD doesn't mean you need to be watched like a hawk.

"For the people who live in the fringe, it seemed more appealing to opt out of society completely rather than to try to correct the problem from within, *like I intend to do*," Nita says (emphasis mine). What Nita doesn't appear to realize is that by bombing the Bureau, she's no longer trying to change the system from within; she's become an Insurgent, attacking from the outside to destroy it. Furthermore, it's revealed the rebels weren't after the memory serum at all, but the death serum. They were prepared to kill innocents, the same way the Bureau actively participated in the deaths of innocents inside the city limits. Neither their methods nor their results were any better than the Bureau's.

Sounds like nearly equal footing to me.

WHERE DOES TRIS FIT IN?

Since Tris, Tobias, and their crew end up fighting against the Bureau, basically finishing Nita's work, I think it's safe to include them on the side of the rebels, even if they disagree with how the rebels go about things. But—and this may be a tough question because Tris *is* the hero of the story—is it really any better for her to erase the memory of the Bureau employees before they can do the same to the residents of Chicago?

Tris admits that the entire Bureau compound can't possibly know what their leaders have done, but she's willing to erase their identities anyway, the very thing she condemns the Bureau for wanting to do in Chicago. Tris says in regard to the Bureau's plan for a total reset, "It's not sacrifice if it's someone *else's* life you're giving away, it's just evil." But then she does exactly that—sacrifice the memories of everyone at the Bureau to save the people in the city—even after Tobias tries to talk her out of it. All of those people in the compound are now simply gone.

Tris argues that the Bureau doesn't want to stop the revolution in the city to save lives, but to save their experiment. Isn't that the same thing? Especially in the long term. The whole goal of the Bureau is to restore order to a semi-lawless world.

The Bureau, evolving *slightly* on a moral level, wants to reset everyone in the city in order to save lives (and, admittedly, the experiment). I say *evolving* since it wasn't that long ago they decided it was easier to wipe out the Abnegation to maintain order. But Tris sees the idea of a memory wipe as equivalent to murder. Taking away someone's identity is taking away who they are, and thus their entire life. I really can't argue with that. Then Tris readily plans to—and accomplishes—wiping the memories and identities of everyone in the Bureau. What is worse: Erasing memories in order to neutralize the brewing war inside Chicago, or erasing the memories of thousands of Bureau employees to stop the memory erasure in Chicago, and then have the war happen anyway?

Yes, Tris does an awful thing—the equivalent of mass murder, according to her—but what would've happened if she hadn't? Would the rebels have eventually succeeded with their death serum? Maybe. Would Chicago have fallen, most of its citizens victim to the internal wars and uprisings? Probably.

In this, Tris isn't so unlike the Bureau. She is willing to sacrifice for the greater good—*her* greater good. What she does is terrible, but it saves the people she loves and believes in most. Which is all she wanted. Trapped in a bad situation with no good options, she makes what she feels is the best choice, and that is all that can be expected from a real human being.

SO WHO'S WORSE?

This wouldn't be a very good smackdown if I just said there are pros and cons to both sides, but didn't pick one as the greater of two evils. While reading *Allegiant*, and while writing the beginning of this essay, I was pro-Bureau. But while I think the Bureau is on the right side of things, I can't get behind them. Probably for the same reasons that Tris couldn't: their end does not justify their means.

So I'm going to say my heart lies with the rebels' cause, but not with them specifically, terrorists that they are. I don't think the Bureau was ever going to give the GDs a chance to prove that the experiment wasn't necessary. Amar says it best: "Genes aren't everything . . . People, even genetically damaged people, make choices. That's what matters." Yes, Amar. Yes, it does. This very idea is what the Bureau is afraid of most.

Caleb, for all his faults, holds on to this one nugget of wisdom from Natalie Prior: "She said that everyone has some evil inside them, and the first step to loving anyone is to recognize the same evil in ourselves, so we're able to forgive them." But forgiving GDs for their part in the Purity Wars isn't something the Bureau seems capable of. GDs would never have been given a chance to rise above. And as we see, they do rise above. Chicago has a bright future at the end of *Allegiant*, even with pesky things like the need for policemen and politicians (can I get an UGH?).

At the same time, I can't ignore the Bureau's logic. I think there is something to genetic damage. In the broken world of *Divergent*, they've been searching for order for

seven long generations. Would the Bureau really have spent
all those centuries studying GDs if there wasn't something
to study? What's the benefit? "Control, maybe?" Nita offers. I don't know. I want to believe there has to be some
kind of onward progression—an insanely slow progression, yes—to allow an experiment like that to continue for
so many years. Otherwise, wouldn't it have been shut down
by the government centuries ago as an unnecessary cost?
But we all know people don't like change, and for a system
as ingrained as the Bureau, where people are *raised* to work
there from birth . . . well, maybe they would've kept at it for
seven more generations, and seven more after that.

Deep down I want to believe that the Bureau does not
hate the genetically damaged as much as Nita thinks they
do. They let the GDs work on their airplanes, for crying
out loud! Would you let someone you thought was inferior
work on your airplane? No, you would not. You'd trust that
job to the most competent person you knew. So it's sad to
see the Bureau not trust GDs to hold the highest positions
of power in their organization. It makes no sense, and only
weakens their stance.

That's one of the reasons I hate the Bureau. I wish they
were better. They have the capacity to be better. After seven
generations, maybe it was time to give up and simply let people *live*. If the Bureau were destroyed, and no one had seen
the Edith Prior video, I think Chicago would've been just
fine. Tris and Tobias would've figured out a way to neutralize Evelyn and Marcus, and their tiny little world would've
chugged right along. Imperfect, not without bloodshed, and
perhaps only until enough Divergents came along to render
the old system obsolete, but the seeds for democracy were
already there in the hearts of people like Tris Prior.

What I want to see is the story after Divergent. Can peace last? What would the next thing we found wrong with each other be? Only Veronica Roth can know.

Maybe the Bureau just reminds me too much of the current dystopia we're living in, a nation where the citizens are spied on and controlled, albeit through things like laws and the distribution of wealth rather than serums.

Perhaps once upon a time the Bureau was a necessary evil, in those precarious days after the Purity War, when America truly was teetering on the brink of total annihilation. But not anymore.

We know now that there is more than one way to handle the effects of genetic damage—the trait-based factions were one option—and it doesn't have to involve breeding humans back to genetic "perfection" over a number of generations.

Tobias, a genetically damaged boy who finds he can grow, he can change, and he can hold on to those changes because they're all that's left of the love of his life, is proof of that.

After pumping gas for nine years to put himself through college, Dan Krokos, now twenty-eight, dropped out to write full-time. He is currently hard at work on three separate projects: the final stop for Miranda North in the False Memory series, the next adventure for thirteen-year-old Mason Stark in The Planet Thieves series, and his first adult thriller. All of Dan's books have been optioned for film or television, and False Memory *recent-ly won the International Thriller Writer's Award for best Young Adult book. He enjoys riding his Harley, playing MMORPGs, and drinking coffee.*

If he had to choose a faction, he'd choose Dauntless. They have the most fun. But he'd go with Amity if they were into zip-lining and jumping into nets and stuff.

Are factions good or bad? It's a debate that comes up many times in the Divergent trilogy, including two notable occasions in Allegiant: inside Tris' city, as the Allegiant discuss their desire to reinstate the factions, and outside it, when David attributes Chicago's success to the faction system. But neither time does the series offer up a definitive judgment. All we know for sure is that, at least in the world of Divergent, factions are effective . . . if sometimes at great cost to individual freedom. Here, Julia Karr takes on the benefits of belonging, the shortcomings of segregation, and the evils to which division and exclusion can leave us open.

FACTIONS: THE GOOD, THE BAD, AND THE UGLY

JULIA KARR

The heat of a summer afternoon turns oppressive, and even though the sun still shines brightly, the atmosphere is as dark and charged as if storm clouds were gathering. Streets fill with military vehicles and soldiers. Shots ring out. A general and his wife lie murdered in their garden—both shot in the back, execution-style. Another military leader is dragged away from his new wife as they're embarking on their honeymoon and shot dead. A journalist is gunned down; a political rival is hacked to death; numerous high-ranking military, religious, and political leaders are arrested and die by firing squad.

Though almost eerily similar to the simulation-controlled Dauntless massacre of unsuspecting Abnegation leaders, this was a real event. In his nonfiction book *In the Garden of Beasts*, about American ambassador to Germany

William Dodd during Adolph Hitler's ascension to power, author Erik Larson describes the chilling scene that unfolded in Berlin on June 30, 1934, at Hitler's order—an event that came to be known as the Night of the Long Knives.

When Jeanine orders the deaths of the Abnegation leaders, she does so without mercy and with the coldhearted intention of removing anyone who might try to thwart her purpose—a purpose that included complete control over the factions and a government of her own design, over which she would rule. Her plan, like Hitler's, could not have succeeded without highly trained, tightly controlled factions of soldiers at her disposal—in Hitler's case, the SS and Gestapo; in Jeanine's, the simulation-controlled Dauntless.

I had just finished reading *In the Garden of Beasts* when I picked up *Divergent*, and I was immediately struck by the similarities between fiction and real life. Both books point out the dangers of blind obedience to any faction, group, or leader. And both show how easy it is to manipulate people who follow a leader unquestioningly (whether because they truly believe their leader is infallible or because they happen to be simulation controlled).

Factions—smaller groups within a larger organization that share a common goal—can be dangerous. The factionless in Chicago are well aware of this. Daily they deal with a lack of basic human necessities, like proper clothing, adequate housing, nutritional food, and medical care, just because they couldn't or didn't want to belong. But the faction system in the Divergent trilogy is also responsible for estranging families, tearing apart friendships, ignoring intolerance and bullying, and suppressing the human spirit—not just expelling or killing anyone who can't, or won't, live up to the demands of whichever faction they are in.

Unfortunately, all this happens in the real world, too.

However, I'm getting ahead of myself. In order to better understand how groups go from good, to bad, to downright awful, we need to first look at what leads people to gather together with like-minded individuals in the first place.

THE GOOD: BEING IN A GROUP

It's human nature to gravitate toward people who like the same kinds of things that we do. It's also empowering and affirming to be part of a group with others whose beliefs are in sync with your own. This is why there are clubs, political parties, and all kinds of different groups, formal and informal, organized around shared experience or shared interests. Spending time with people with similar experiences or values validates the way we think and feel about ourselves and the world around us. It gives us an anchor in what can often feel like storm-tossed seas of life options and emotions.

In the Chicago experiment, we originally learn that the factions are organized around shared beliefs and shared aptitudes. Later, of course, we learn it's also organized around shared identity: similarly modified genetics. So it makes a lot of sense that the Choosing Ceremony takes place at sixteen. Teens are at a point in life when they are beginning to question the values they grew up with and look for their own place in the world. At sixteen, I was searching for my own identity, as were most of my friends. Tris' secret longing as she watches the Dauntless arrive at school each day reminded me of my own desire to become someone different than the small-town girl I was. Whereas Tris aligns herself with Dauntless, I gravitated to the counterculture of the 1960s. Both choices were extremely different than our backgrounds, and both offered a feeling of belonging and a camaraderie with people with whom we could identify. When you find a group that supports who you feel you are inside, you're eager to be a part of it.

Besides identity, another reason to be part of a group is common interests and shared goals. You might join a drama club because you're interested in theater and want to be involved in a play. You might not be able to (or even want to) act, but you might have a knack for or really enjoy set building, costuming, or makeup. In groups like this, everyone adds value, whether they're onstage or behind the scenes. Even though their talents (their aptitudes, you could say) are diverse, they are all integral to the group, and especially its ability to achieve its goal: putting on that play.

Very frequently, a united group can achieve things a single person cannot. Historically, trailblazers like the Puritan colonists or America's early westward-bound pioneers joined together to travel and carve out settlements in foreign surroundings. Although the Puritans had a shared goal of religious freedom, the settlers had varied reasons for traveling west. However, everyone within each group shared the need for safety and survival. That collective need bonded the community because they all knew they were more likely to survive if they helped each other and acted as a connected whole than if the members thought and acted only as it concerned them individually.

Another benefit of joining a group is that it can provide structure and guidance, a safe haven where things make sense. Before Jeanine's failed coup, faction members in Divergent knew both their roles within their faction and their faction's role within the larger community. After Evelyn and the factionless take over control of the city, it is not surprising that some people would want to return to the familiarity of the faction system—or that they would form another group, the Allegiant, so quickly. The faction system was flawed, but it helped people feel secure in the knowledge of who they were and what their purpose was. Losing that is never easy. "And I'm not sure how Dauntless I really am, anyway, now that the factions are gone," Tris thinks in *Allegiant*. "I feel a strange little ache at the thought . . . some things are hard to let go of."

Belonging is a powerful thing. It can create bonds so powerful and passionate that you can easily feel a closer kinship with a chosen group than with your birth family. In Tris' world, you can see this feeling (and see this feeling being reinforced) in the motto "faction before blood." She and her newfound friends become as close as, if not closer than, her family ever was.

THE BAD: BEING OUT OF A GROUP

There's an unavoidable downside that comes with all those upsides: for a group to exist, there has to be something that makes some people "in" and other people "out." Segregation, by its very nature, focuses on exclusion rather than inclusion, and that comes with the very real risk of not only setting person against person, but group against group— no matter how respectable, principled, and ethical a group might be.

People who remain "in" the group develop biases against those who are not a part of the group, and act accordingly. For those on the outside, the manifestations of these biases run the gamut from the mildly uncomfortable to incredibly harsh.

We see one of the milder manifestations of this kind of bias in the Chicago experiment early in *Divergent*, when Tris transfers to Dauntless and is immediately nicknamed Stiff. "Stiff" is the term other factions use to talk disdainfully about Abnegation. There's a stereotype and accompanying slur for every faction: an Erudite is a Nose; a Dauntless is an adrenaline junkie; a Candor is a smart-mouth; Amities are "banjo strumming softies." They're all evidence of the prejudices that have arisen from the city's segregation into factions. In Tris' city, where the factions largely live separately, the expression of these prejudices mostly remains verbal. In our world, though, similar prejudices—between different races or sexualities or even groups like nerds and jocks—lead to violence all the time.

Those inside the group, or who want to be there, don't avoid the negative consequences of faction life either. There is often a price one must pay in order to belong—and I don't mean membership dues.

In order to join some groups, initiates must perform certain rituals that allow group leaders to evaluate their suitability to join. Sororities and fraternities on college campuses have rush weeks to screen students who wish to join them, then take on prospective members as pledges. Although many of the pledging rituals are relatively harmless (tending more toward having the initiates embarrass and/ or demean themselves publicly), there are times when these customs become far more dangerous. Hazing of prospective members has, on occasion, led to serious physical harm or death—much like in the case of the Dauntless initiate who fails to make the roof when jumping from the train.

Despite these risks, many people continue to take part in initiations and hazings because their desire to get into a certain group is more powerful than their misgivings and fears. Tris herself stuffs down any emotion surrounding the girl's death, rationalizing that being Dauntless is dangerous and people dying is an unavoidable aspect of her new chosen life. That risk is just the cost of being Dauntless.

That need to belong also affects members' behavior. When you want to be a part of something badly enough, you'll do a lot—maybe even anything—to belong, and that willingness to change your behavior in order to become part of a group can be exploited. During Dauntless initiation, the low initiate acceptance rate creates so much rivalry within the group that people like Peter are willing to maim and kill in order to remove obstacles that might keep them from being admitted to the group—which is what Dauntless leadership intends to happen. The desperation to become Dauntless drives initiates not only to get better at positive skills like throwing knives and overcoming fear, but also to become more brutal. And those who are not as strong or as ruthless can get hurt.

Even once you're accepted into a group, things don't necessarily get any easier or better. There are those individuals who initially feel like they belong, but as their new group's dynamic becomes clearer, they're no longer so sure. I never entirely embraced being a "turn on, tune in, drop out" hippie in the 1960s. I hung out on the fringe of the group with the people I felt closest to, never completely fitting in. When reading *Divergent*, I never felt like Tris and Tobias fit into Dauntless 100 percent, either—though they have their reasons for staying, just as I had my reasons for staying on the edges of hippie-dom.

The pressure to behave in a certain way also doesn't go away; you have to adhere to the group's standards (of behavior, or dress, or whatever else), or else lose your place. If you can't conform, then you're out—and even for those who don't feel like the group is a perfect fit, that can be a powerful threat. The worst kind of "out" in Tris' world is to fail your initiation and end up factionless, which Tris (and everyone else) believes is, as Tris says in *Divergent*, "a fate worse than death." To be left in the world without the support and structure of your faction would be a difficult adjustment indeed. Especially given that Tris' world requires estrangement from family and friends when you switch factions—the way many cults require their members to cut off contact with anyone from their former lives.

The Peoples Temple, formed by the charismatic James "Jim" Jones, encouraged new members to break familial ties and end prior friendships. Isolated from outside support, initiates were worn down by sleep deprivation, constant lectures, intimidation, and abuse until they were completely dependent on the church for their very lives. (Doesn't sound much different than Dauntless initiation in some ways, does it?) In the end, over 900 of those lives were ended in Jonestown, Guyana, November 18, 1978, at the instruction of the Peoples Temple leaders—either by mass suicide or murder.

Which brings us to where things get ugly—to where groups become factions, and factions get scary.

THE UGLY: FACTIONS AND THEIR MANIPULATION AND USE

Earlier, I defined factions as smaller groups with common goals inside larger organizations. But there is a little bit more to it than that. Factions are usually formed in opposition to something—like how the Divergent trilogy's factions are formed in opposition to things such as dishonesty and ignorance and violence. Except instead of just opposing certain ideas, most real-world factions form against groups of people. And when those factions are led by someone who has no problem justifying any means to attain their ends—whether those ends match the greater faction's or not—they can become deadly.

The trouble often starts when one group feels threatened, endangered, or believes that another group is in some way undermining theirs. If that happens, they may turn against the offending group. They may become a faction.

Prejudices are built on difference. That's not ideal, but it's hard to avoid, and as long as those different groups are equal in power, most people aren't really getting hurt. When two groups are forced to compete against each other for resources like money or power—the way Hitler claimed the "pure" Germans and Jews were—that's when they become factions. And when one faction wins—when one faction gains power over the other—difference becomes an excuse to prevent the other group from having the same opportunities and access to resources as the dominant group. The more powerful group's prejudice is institutionalized.

We see it in the Chicago experiment with the factionless. Faction members appear to live comfortable lives with plenty of food and readily available housing. The factionless—those who couldn't cut it in a faction—are not so lucky. They struggle to obtain enough to eat, much less clothes to wear and comfortable places to sleep, and no one in the factions does much about it; the Abnegation are the only ones who seem to care at all. The factionless are not just different from faction members, they're less worthy. Even though many of them

have jobs—"the work no one else wants to do" (*Divergent*)—
they don't get the same access to the city's resources as faction
members do because they don't deserve it.

The situation outside the city is similar. In *Allegiant*, we
are introduced to two new factions: GPs, or the genetically
pure, and GDs, or the genetically damaged. The Bureau's
subtle (in the compound) and not-so-subtle (in the fringe)
treatment of GDs as inferior to GPs is yet another example
of what happens when one group has power over another.
GDs are told they are equals, yet they live every day with inequalities. A murder of a GD by a GP might be prosecuted
as a case of manslaughter, if it's prosecuted at all. GDs are
not allowed to move into positions of authority in the Bureau, included in decision-making, or allowed to have leadership roles—those are reserved for GPs. (Although the GD
are allowed to be useful, people like Nita know they are considered second-class citizens and can never rise further than
they already have.) And those GDs who live in the fringe
lack as many services and rights as the factionless do in Chicago. Even the term used to describe them reflects the imbalance of power: they're not just genetically different, they're
genetically damaged. The very name implies inferiority. No
matter how supposedly scientific the evidence behind the
Bureau's reasoning is—human nature made the separation
between GP and GD a rift that eventually became a chasm.

To people like David, the GD are not fully human; they
are merely damaged goods, or in the case of the GD living
in Chicago, lab rats. Their memories, identities, and lives
are expendable. As Tris puts it, they are "just containers
of genetic material—just GDs, valuable for the corrected
genes they pass on, and not for the brains in their heads or
the hearts in their chests" (*Allegiant*).

Sadly, you don't have to look too far in our own society to see inequities among groups theoretically based on genetics—those between races and ethnicities. In fact, it was impossible for me to read about the genetically pure and damaged without thinking of how ethnicity and race are used as the basis of so many spoken and unspoken barriers in our world. It's way too easy to come up with examples of groups who were—and still are—discriminated against, in ways both large and small: slaves and Native Americans in the United States, Aborigines in Australia, Roma in Europe—the list goes on and on. But, since *In the Garden of Beasts* is on my mind, I have only to look as far as Nazi Germany to see the terrible places that kind of pure/impure thinking can lead. Hitler's stated purpose was to form a pure Aryan nation. (Reminiscent of David's genetically pure, isn't it?)

Often, such prejudices, and the reasoning they hinge on, simmer just under the surface. But an unscrupulous leader can bring these prejudices to a boil and manipulate them to meet his or her own needs.

You can see this at work in *Divergent* with Jeanine and the Erudite. Jeanine's fear of Abnegation revealing the Edith Prior video, which could lead to the dissolution of the faction system and a loss of power for her as faction leader, leads her to spread lies about Abnegation, saying that they are hoarding food and supplies, and slandering Tris' father and other Abnegation leaders with the goal of turning the other factions against them. She clearly convinced the Dauntless leadership—and who knows how many more?

This was the same tactic used by Hitler against the Jews prior to, and throughout, World War II. Unlike Jeanine's devious undermining of Abnegation through rumors and innuendoes, Hitler was never subtle about his anti-Semitic rhetoric. His views that Jews hated the white race, stole from the Germans, became wealthy on the backs of working German people, etc., was initially spread via his autobiographical manifesto, *Mein Kampf,* and once in power, Hitler openly blamed the Jews for everything from Germany's loss of the World War I to 1929's German Depression. He tapped into Germans' dissatisfaction and their established prejudices against the Jews, and used it to build, then solidify, his own power.

It wasn't just the Jews. Whoever was deemed unsuitable (and Hitler's list was long—the Roma, homosexuals, the disabled, certain religions . . .) was targeted, first through innuendo and rumor and then through laws like the "Aryan clause" in Germany's civil service laws, which banned Jews from holding government offices. And then there was the Gleichschaltung, or "Coordination," which "[brought] citizens, government ministries, universities, and cultural and social institutions in line with National Socialist beliefs and attitudes" (*In the Garden of Beasts*). This was the Nazification of Germany, whereby all organizations (including religious, educational, and civic) were either brought in line with Nazi policies or became forbidden and were disbanded. Workers unions were dissolved, no other political parties were allowed, and there were compulsory organizations (such as Hitler Youth, Labor Service, and Young Maidens) that started in childhood and progressed to adulthood. If you were in (which was mandatory for all who qualified), there was no way out.

At the street level, the Coordination worked much like Erudite's smear campaign against Abnegation, or against the Divergent: spread evidence to support existing prejudices (the Stiffs were being greedy, hoarding resources the other factions needed; the Divergent were dangerous) and watch human nature take over. *In the Garden of Beasts* relates the "amorphous anxiety" that changed German lives "like a pale mist that slipped into every crevice . . . You began to think differently about whom you met for lunch . . . In the most casual of circumstances you spoke carefully and paid attention to those around you." Fear of being identified with anything forbidden turned friends against friends, and families turned against their own—much like Caleb turned against Tris.

Although Jeanine's attempted destruction of Abnegation is horrific, it is noteworthy that none of the other factions step up to defend Abnegation. Amity flat out refuses to help except as "a safe house for members of all factions" (*Insurgent*). Distracted by Jeanine's campaign against Abnegation, the factions lack the willingness, or foresight, to recognize that what happened to Abnegation could just as easily happen to them. And I can't help but compare this to the rest of the free world, which initially refused to censure or condemn Hitler's actions. World leaders stuck their collective heads in the sand until Hitler's atrocities could no longer be ignored.

Leaders like Jeanine and Hitler have been around since humankind began, as the founders of the experimental cities must have known. Why else would they have invented the memory serum to reset experiments gone bad? I doubt that the Bureau GP ever recognized in themselves the same cruel and self-serving actions—the same manipulation of others for their own ends, made justifiable by their prejudices—that they were using the memory serum to prevent. Certainly David didn't seem to—before Tris erased his memory.

ARE FACTIONS NECESSARY?

Of course, one way to prevent manipulative, self-serving leaders from exploiting factions' prejudices would be to get rid of factions altogether. As John Dickinson, one of America's founding fathers, wrote in 1768, "By uniting we stand, by dividing we fall." Is there any reason not to try to prevent factions from forming in the first place?

Despite the Bureau's claim that Chicago is the most successful experimental city because of the factions, I think the factions were the biggest flaw in their design. Chicago may have lasted longer than the experiments without factions, but it, too, eventually falls apart—and no doubt would have sooner, without the Bureau's serum interventions.

Dividing people into groups, and then allowing those groups to evolve into egocentric entities whose members have little or no respect for anyone outside of the group, can only result in conflict and further separation between the groups. This is as true inside Chicago as it is outside it.

What's missing from the faction system—what the faction system makes difficult, if not impossible—is empathy for fellow humans. In order for a government to be successful, all factions—whether the Divergent trilogy's factions or those in our own world—need to work together, respecting the strengths and differences of each.

Integration—getting to know different people and exploring new thoughts—is a key component in increasing respect and tolerance for others and the best chance of combatting the group-based prejudices we naturally tend toward. In the Divergent trilogy, there's no better example of integration than Tris. She's fearless, but her selfless Abnegation tendencies soften the harsh edges of Dauntless, and her Erudite intelligence gives her the ability to reason, question, and modify her beliefs even in the midst of life-threatening situations. In one respect, the Bureau was right about the Divergent being able to save them: the qualities that make Tris Divergent are the very ones her world needs most.

It's human nature to establish groups. Evelyn tells Tobias, "People always organize into groups. That's a fact of our existence" (*Allegiant*). Sympathetic natures attract us to each other. But in any successful group, it's the inclusion of and compassion for all its members that truly allow the group to flourish. When a group devolves into cliques and factions, it becomes disempowered. Had the Chicago experiment continued to appreciate the diversity and individual strengths of all the factions, it wouldn't have fallen apart. But fighting the baser human tendencies—to aggrandize oneself and one's faction at the expense of others—is a continual struggle.

A world tempered with empathy, kindness, and respect can only be achieved through vigilance, mindfulness, and close scrutiny of those in power. It's not easy, but nothing worth having is.

Julia Karr *is the author of two teen dystopian novels,* XVI *and its sequel,* Truth. *She lives in Bloomington, Indiana, with her cats, Frankenstein and Esmerelda. If she had to choose a faction she'd choose Amity, since her free time is spent keeping peace between the cats and tending her garden.*

Janine Spendlove is not only a YA author, but also a Marine, who as of this writing works as a legislative liaison to the US House of Representatives. So she's in an especially good position to offer insight on Dauntless' devolution from its original principles to what it becomes under Jeanine's influence—and what both the Bureau and Dauntless itself could have done differently to prevent that change.

THE DOWNFALL OF DAUNTLESS

Janine K. Spendlove

War is too serious a matter to entrust to military men.
—Georges Clemenceau

The point of civilian control is to make security subordinate to the larger purposes of a nation, rather than the other way around. The purpose of the military is to defend society, not to define it.
—Richard Kohn

What makes a good man commit an evil act? How does a faction with high-minded ideals of "ordinary acts of bravery" and "the courage that drives one person to stand up for another" devolve into chaos, violence, and murder? Do genetics control a person's acts, or can training and personal choice overcome "natural programming"? How does the physically strongest faction become the tool of another?

In the world of Divergent we are given a look into the five complementary faction societies that make up Tris' city: Candor—peace through truth; Amity—peace through avoidance of conflict; Abnegation—peace through selflessness; Erudite—peace through knowledge; and Dauntless—peace through bravery. And yet, despite their noble principles, this "perfect society" is rotting and crumbling from within. Like a row of dominos, all it takes to bring down this balanced society is the fall of one faction.

That faction is Dauntless.

The faction known for courage, bravery, and fearlessness, Dauntless was founded by those who blamed fear for the world's problems. Dauntless' objective is to combat cowardice by training its members to act in the face of fear—not necessarily to rid themselves of fear, but to embrace it and overcome it. Though it was founded upon the highest ideal of defense of those who cannot defend themselves, it becomes clear during Tris' initiation in *Divergent* that Dauntless has drifted quite far from its core belief of attaining peace through freedom from fear. In fact, peace no longer seems to be a goal for Dauntless at all.

This is perfectly illustrated in the scene in *Divergent* where Dauntless initiates Al and Will are fighting, and massive, yet gentlehearted, Al is unwillingly beating Will to a pulp. Al wants the fight to end since it's clear he has won/will win, and as their instructor, Tobias offers the option of Will conceding the match to prevent more unnecessary violence, suggesting that "a brave man acknowledges the strength of others." Not only does Will refuse to concede the fight, but Dauntless leader Eric says, "In the *new* rules, no one concedes . . . A brave man never surrenders."

How did this happen? How did Dauntless shift its focus from defense to offense? From killing to murder?

By looking at the real-world military and related psychological studies, some answers become readily apparent.

Dauntless' founding principles are similar to those currently held by modern-day military and police forces such as the United States Marine Corps—"Honor, Courage, Commitment" (the first principles I, along with every other Marine, learned upon joining the Corps) and the Los Angeles Police Department—"To Protect and to Serve." Though trained, structured, and administered like a military force, Dauntless was originally used to patrol not only the edges of the city, but also the factionless areas as a police force (until Abnegation voted to have them stop)—which inherently leads to a conflict of interest.

Military forces are not civilians, and once a civilian dons a military uniform they give up many rights and privileges that citizens of society are allowed. They no longer have some forms of freedom of speech (i.e., members of the military cannot publicly speak out against the President, their Commander in Chief). They cannot "quit" their jobs when they'd like (most have a minimum contracted obligation of four years), they can be charged and found guilty of things that negatively impact the good order and discipline of a unit (such as adultery), and they are held to strict weight, grooming, and physical fitness standards (if you are overweight or cannot pass the annual physical fitness test, you will be administratively separated from the military). Military members are even held to a different justice system and standards (the Uniform Code of Military Justice, in the United States). A military's purpose is to take over when politics fail; they go forward into battle when words no longer work. Conversely, police officers are civilians, tasked with peacekeeping, not warfighting. Based on why Dauntless was formed, and how it has been utilized in the past, Dauntless' role in this society is to be peacekeepers. Yet they are trained for battle and war, which leaves a void that, in lieu of any other guidance or employment of said skills, is often filled by reckless thrill seeking, and eventually, in *Divergent*, something much worse.

Dauntless initiates don't arrive trained and ready to kill. Generally, humans have a natural aversion to killing other humans. Knowing this, it should come as no surprise that without proper training to overcome this instinct, most soldiers—or, as in this case, Dauntless initiates—will not automatically or willingly kill the "enemy." Think of Tris at the beginning of *Divergent*, who, given her Abnegation background, would have found it difficult to hurt another living creature even at the expense of her own life. Yet by the end of the book she is able to, without hesitation, shoot a friend in the head in self-defense. This was learned, not natural, behavior.

People generally assume that troops in battle instinctively respond to attack with a counterattack or that in a kill-or-be-killed situation, soldiers will choose to kill. This is not the case. One hundred fifty years ago, after the Battle of Gettysburg, thousands of rifles were found on the battlefield filled to the top with wad. What this tells us is that soldiers had pretended to fire, then reloaded their rifles until the barrels were absolutely full. Interviews conducted with thousands of American soldiers during World War II by Army historian S. L. A. Marshall revealed that as many as 75 percent of soldiers never fired their weapons during combat.

So if humans have a natural aversion to killing, how do we overcome this? Because we do manage to kill each other. A lot.

The answer is psychology, exploitation of our natural

instinct toward herd mentality, and, of course, training, training, and more training. Tried and true practices such as dehumanizing the victim (take a look at old WWII propaganda posters on both sides of the war: the Japanese were frequently depicted by Americans as less-than-human apes, and the Americans were depicted by the Japanese as cannibalistic monsters) and placing distance between the killer and the victim (e.g., via bombs, long-range weapons) are very effective, but more than that, the training incorporated by the military has made a huge difference. After Marshall's findings were published following WWII, the US military radically reformed its training process to more effectively prepare troops for combat.

While the US Marine Corps had always trained and enforced the ideal of "every Marine a Rifleman" (such that cooks, drivers, or administrators do not hesitate to pick up a rifle and fight alongside the infantry when needed), it was a radically foreign concept to the other branches of service, particularly the Army, and they needed to adjust their training practices drastically.

Bull's-eye targets were swapped out for pop-up human-shaped targets to accustom the recruits to firing at human forms. More realistic combat training scenarios were devised to prepare the recruits mentally for the chaos of war, and large simulations/exercises/war games were completed to teach even the smallest unit leader how to think and adjust to the ever-changing situation in combat. Even something as seemingly innocuous as teaching new recruits to yell "kill" when closing with and destroying the enemy psychologically prepared them for what they'd have to do. The ultimate objective was to make killing an automatic response in combat.

As Tobias says in *Allegiant*, "The physical technique is important . . . but it's mostly a mental game . . . You don't just practice the shooting, you also practice the focus. And then, when you're in a situation where you're fighting for your life, the focus will be so ingrained that it will happen naturally."

And it works, both in Dauntless and the US military. Interviews with American soldiers during the Vietnam War showed that nearly all the soldiers shot at enemies during firefights.

In this respect, Dauntless is operating as it should. Their training is appropriately preparing the initiates to use violence against other human beings when necessary. But that's not all training is for—and this is where the Dauntless training goes awry.

As in any sort of physically demanding task, there will be some natural attrition through either physical injury or a desire not to continue—generally no more than 10 percent in a standard military recruit-training environment. These losses are actually a good thing, in that those who remain are the ones most capable of fulfilling the role they are being trained for. Rigorous training also creates what will ultimately become a very effective and cohesive fighting force. But Dauntless takes things in their initiation to a counterproductive extreme by weeding out over 50 percent of their initiates. "You chose us," Eric tells Tris' initiate class in *Divergent*. "Now we have to choose you."

What the Dauntless leaders have failed to realize (or perhaps they just ignore it because of the "new rules") is that ultimately troops do not fight for the "greater good," or for their country or whatever "great purpose" is placed before them. No, troops fight for their team—for their brothers- and sisters-in-arms. They fight for each other because they are family—a family whose ties are thicker than blood. Those ties have been forged over months, if not years, of shared hardship and triumph, shared culture, and shared purpose, and as such, those bonds are unbreakable.

Dauntless has removed, through purposeful attrition, any sort of team mentality or desire to work together. They have removed any familial bonds or ties. Every member is looking out for themselves, not for their fellow Dauntless.

We can ascertain from what Tobias tells Tris about how much Dauntless has changed just since he transferred there that this was not how Dauntless was originally envisioned. Initially, Dauntless was probably much like our modern-day military, where nearly anyone who physically qualifies for boot camp will be transformed into a soldier, sailor, Marine, or airman. Dauntless' reason for the harsh cuts and attrition may have been that they only wanted the best, but what ended up happening was that they wound up with the most ruthless and brutal—those who would stab anyone, including fellow Dauntless, in the back to advance themselves.

The motto of the Marine Corps is Semper Fidelis (often shortened to Semper Fi), which means "Always Faithful," and is exemplified by the handling of Marine recruits in recruit training. Marines are faithful to the Corps, and the Corps is faithful to its Marines. The Marine Corps Recruit Depot (MCRD) has a banner over its entrance that states "WE MAKE MARINES." And they do. As opposed to Dauntless' attrition rate of more than 50 percent, the MCRD's attrition rate is only about 9 percent from recruitment to graduation from boot camp. By graduation, these new Marines have worked hard with each other and have learned to depend on each other, to trust each other with their very lives throughout the most stressful and physically demanding situations they have ever faced. A Marine is willing to put her life on the line because she knows her fellow Marines would do the same for her in a heartbeat. Marine recruits leave MCRD transformed into the most effective warfighting force in the world.

Why would someone willingly choose to put themselves through that? What attracts people to the Marine Corps? It's still, of all the branches, the most difficult and exclusive to get into. As a current recruitment poster says, "We'd promise you sleep deprivation, mental torment, and muscles so sore you'll puke, but we don't like to sugar-coat things." As with Dauntless, the Marine Corps is a place where young people go to prove themselves or to show that they are tough. Many are attracted by the challenge they know the Marines will give them. Others don't like to be told "no" or "you can't." There is an allure to being part of an exclusive group, to being part of the best of the best, but there must be a team aspect to it—a family, a sense of belonging. Otherwise, it will fall apart, or only those who like to fight for the sake of fighting will stick around. By breaking their recruits down, the modern-day military training depots do an excellent job of building their recruits back up together as a family and a cohesive fighting force.

As demonstrated in *Divergent*, Dauntless just breaks their recruits and certainly does not build them back up or instill in them the pride of what they do/what their purpose is. Ask any Marine recruit to recite their Corps values and they can spit them out without hesitation. Ask a member of Dauntless, and I suspect most would be hard-pressed to tell you what their faction even stands for at this point.

Somewhere along the way, Dauntless lost something precious: its heart.

One of the main problems with Dauntless is that, at its core, it exists only for itself. It superficially serves a "higher calling" by patrolling the border, but it no longer does any interior police work (which eventually leads to the faction-less gathering together, rebelling, and eventually destroying Dauntless as a faction). Which means that, ultimately, Dauntless serves no real purpose. What are they defending the city from? Empty fields? There is no visible threat, and because of this, no occasion for the members of Dauntless to utilize the training they have been given, which leads us back once again to the reckless, thrill-seeking behavior mentioned above—zip-lining, hanging over a cliff, jumping from heights, jumping onto and off a moving train.

The factions were originally set up to work independently of each other. Though together they comprised a balanced and functional society, each faction had autonomy and no one faction provided oversight over another. The main danger in allowing a militaristic group (like Dauntless) so much autonomy is that eventually they discard the democratic decision-making process and use physical force to achieve their goals, whatever those goals may be. Our own history is rife with examples: Julius Caesar illegally crossing the Rubicon with the Roman army in 49 B.C., marching on Rome, and eventually becoming dictator in perpetuity—the first domino in the downfall of the Roman Empire and the democracy they held so dear; the Soviets (dominated by the Bolsheviks) overthrowing and taking over from the Russian Provisional Government in 1917's October Revolution, thus paving the way for Joseph Stalin's regime, during which millions lost their lives.

We combat this in real-world democracies by assigning elected civilian leaders oversight of the military. The military retains judicial autonomy and a manner of preserving good order and discipline among its ranks, but elected civilian leaders appoint people to the highest military positions rather than allowing the military to self-select their leaders. For example, general officers in the US military must be vetted, approved, and voted on by the Senate in a confirmation hearing before they can take a major command or assume their next rank.

When people are placed in positions of absolute authority in a closed environment (like a faction) without any form of external oversight or accountability, a pattern often emerges. Behavior that would be considered aberrant in the larger society can become the socially accepted norm. Abuse, brutality, hazing, and violence creep in, eventually sinking roots so deep that the members of the controlling group don't even realize how far they've strayed from their moral center. From the inside, most don't even realize anything is wrong.

That's not the only consequence. American military historian Professor Richard H. Kohn states in his essay on "Civilian Control of the Military" that control of the military by elected civilians is essential because it allows a nation to base its values, purpose, beliefs, and institutions on the popular will rather than the will of the strongest, most ruthless, and power hungry. In order to operate efficiently and work as a cohesive unit, a military organization cannot, by its very nature, be a democratic society. Orders must be obeyed and acted upon immediately with no time for debate. Whereas if the most efficient, expeditious route to action is taken in the general populace, often the "little guy"—the weak, the small, the timid, those who have just as much right to representation and having their needs heard and met—gets trampled and ignored.

Essentially, without civilian oversight, the very people the military is sworn to defend become marginalized and eventually forgotten.

This is where proper civilian oversight could have proven beneficial for Dauntless. Instead of being sequestered in its own space to devolve into the violence-ruled enclave it became, where the most vicious and strongest survived to lead and set the tone, an altruistic, selfless faction like Abnegation could have provided guidance and policies and prevented that from happening. While Abnegation *is* in charge of making overall laws for the city, the individual factions still appear to be autonomous in how they administer things within their own groups, with no direct oversight from other factions. Cross-faction oversight would have been a much-needed check and balance that, in fact, all the factions could have used from each other. Because without formal civilian oversight, Dauntless was left with a vacuum that allowed the most power-hungry and ruthless members within it to take control, which made it possible for Jeanine and the Erudite faction she led to influence and utilize Dauntless for their own ends.

There is a general understanding among democratic nations that "civilianizing" the military—meaning having an all-volunteer military force instead of drafted troops—is the best means of preserving the loyalty of the armed forces toward civilian authorities. It prevents the development of an independent "caste" of warriors that might see itself as existing fundamentally apart from the rest of society. Which is precisely what has happened with Dauntless. They have become a warrior caste with no purpose, and they *need* a purpose. When Jeanine and the Erudite roll in with one, Dauntless leadership is more than happy to oblige.

With Erudite having stepped in, shouldn't Dauntless then have the civilian oversight they clearly need? Technically, yes; realistically, no. If we were to liken Dauntless, Erudite, and Abnegation to their real-world counterparts, they'd match up most closely with the military, the corporate sector (the technological and industrial base), and the government, respectively. Yes, our military and the corporate sector do have a relationship, and a very good relationship at that, but industry does not control or provide oversight of the military. And it shouldn't, because the corporate sector is all about their bottom line. Their primary concern is the revenue to continue their work, not the health and well-being of the civilian populace. The military needs "stuff" (the three "Bs": beans, bullets, and Band-Aids) and the corporate sector provides that "stuff." The government provides the oversight.

What becomes apparent over the course of the events in *Divergent* is that in this society the corporate sector is driving the train on how the military is utilized, and the government is providing absolutely no oversight at all. Erudite, the faction that has goals that are not beneficial to the society as a whole, has control of Dauntless, the faction capable of physically enforcing said goals, and that's a very dangerous combination.

As soon as Erudite's leader, Jeanine, perceived something or someone (in this case Abnegation and the Divergent) as a threat to the fabric and structure of society, she utilized Dauntless to neutralize that threat.

Any given group of people is going to include a percentage of sociopaths—those who kill without conscience (aka murder) and commit what in the US military would be termed as war crimes. In Dauntless, you have a certain type of Erudite transfer.

Because they are genetically engineered to value knowledge above all else and, according to David in *Allegiant*, are lacking in compassion for others, the Erudite are more likely to lack the filter that would prevent a "genetically pure" human (or human from another faction) from killing. So, when Erudites transfer to Dauntless, they have a tendency to become cruel, bullying, conscienceless, and highly intelligent killing machines. In short, sociopaths.

A perfect example of this is Erudite transfer Eric, who seems to take joy not just in causing others pain, but also in resorting to any means necessary to climb to the top of his social sphere—to win or be the best. We know from Tobias that Eric was ruthless in his initiate class. Even two years after graduating, he is constantly gunning for Tobias, viewing him as a rival and threat and looking for a way to permanently remove him despite Tobias having made it very clear he has no desire to move up in the Dauntless ranks.

(Peter isn't an Erudite transfer—he's originally from Candor—but between his Eric-like ruthlessness during initiation and his defection to Erudite in *Insurgent*, it's easy to mistake him for one. In *Divergent*, Peter takes out Edward with a knife to the eye while he sleeps because Edward is at the top of the ranking structure, and then later makes an attempt on Tris' life after it becomes clear she is the next highest-ranked initiate. After all, David says in *Allegiant* that lack of compassion is a flaw of Candor's, too.)

But the blame for Dauntless' devolution cannot solely be placed on Erudite. Others, like Dauntless leader Max, while not (as far as we know) Erudite transfers, were easily influenced and controlled by Jeanine. Max was responsible for changing the training methods to make them more competitive and brutal, as well as appointing Erudite transfer

Eric as a Dauntless leader, at Jeanine's demand, thus assisting her in creating an army she could use to wipe out the Divergent. While it can be assumed that Dauntless was already slowly becoming a more brutal and violent faction due to the lack of civilian oversight and harsh initiate attrition rate, the moment Jeanine placed a target on the Divergent, the priorities of Dauntless changed.

Further evidence of Jeanine and Erudite's influence on Max and Dauntless is the fact that the Dauntless leaders were not only complicit in, but actively a part of, the enslavement of their Dauntless troops' minds and the use of them to murder the peaceful Abnegation faction. No matter how far Dauntless had degraded toward unnecessary violence and brutality, they were not yet at the point where they would attack and murder an entire faction (especially a faction that would not fight back), and Erudite knew this, which is why they put Dauntless, as a whole, under the simulation serum.

But how did Jeanine convince the Dauntless leaders to do what they knew to be morally wrong and act contrary to their faction's manifesto, "We believe in shouting for those who can only whisper, in defending those who cannot defend themselves"? By twisting words and providing what is referred to in the military as "top cover"—an authority they could blame for their actions, the ever-familiar excuse that "I was just doing my job."

In 1961, Yale University psychologist Stanley Milgram conducted a series of social psychology experiments where he measured people's willingness to obey an authority figure who instructed them to perform acts that conflicted with their personal conscience and moral code.

Three individuals were involved in each experiment:

the Experimenter, the one running the experiment; the Teacher, the subject of the experiment (a volunteer); and the Learner, a confederate of the researcher pretending to be a volunteer. The experiment began by taking two volunteers and identifying who would be the Teacher and who would be the Learner, then separating them in different rooms, from which they could communicate but not see each other. The Teacher then asked a series of questions of the Learner, and for every incorrect response given, the Teacher was told to administer a shock to the Learner, with the voltage increasing in 15-volt increments.

Unknown to the Teacher, the Learners were not actually receiving shocks. Once safely in a separate room, the Learner set up a tape recorder that played prerecorded sounds of pain (screams) for each shock level. At a certain level the Learner would also bang on the wall that separated him from the Teacher, and then escalate things by complaining about a heart condition, until eventually ceasing to respond altogether.

Once the Learner stopped responding, most Teachers (the actual test subjects) indicated their desire to stop the experiment and check on the Learner. Some of the Teachers paused earlier, at 135 volts, and began to question the purpose of the experiment. However, *most of those who questioned the experiment continued after being assured that they would not be held responsible.* A few of the Teachers began to show signs of extreme stress (such as nervous laughter) once they heard the screams of pain coming from the Learner. Of the Teachers observed, 65 percent of them took the experiment all the way to the highest shock of 450 volts, despite the Learner's screams and frequent pleas to stop the experiment.

In the experiment, if the Teachers indicated their desire to stop, they were given a succession of verbal prods by the experimenter, in this order:

1. Please *continue*.
2. The experiment requires that you *continue*.
3. It is absolutely essential that you *continue*.
4. You have no other choice, you *must* go on.

If the Teachers still wished to stop after all four successive verbal prods, the experiment was halted. Otherwise, it was stopped after the Teachers had given the maximum 450-volt shock to the Learners three times in succession. Again, *65 percent of the Teachers took the experiment all the way to the end.* Additionally, none of the Teachers who refused to administer the final shocks insisted that the experiment itself be terminated, nor left the room to check the health of the Learner without requesting permission to leave.

We've already established that humans, by their very nature, do not desire to inflict physical pain on each other. So how could this have been the experiment's result? The answer goes back to our tendency to obey authority and the protection authority grants us from being held accountable for our actions.

The results of the study demonstrate that, when provided with a legitimizing ideology and social and institutional support, people are more willing to do things they'd normally consider immoral or wrong. They can rationalize their behavior by saying that because they were under orders, what happens is not really their fault. If an authority is saying it's fine—if the experiment is still happening and hasn't been shut down—it must be okay. It's a natural instinct for people to do what those around them are doing, even if it means doing something they would normally morally oppose, or never consider doing alone.

Six years after these experiments, one of the Teachers/test subjects in the experiment sent a letter to Milgram, explaining why he was glad to have participated despite the stress involved: "While I was a subject in 1964, though I believed that I was hurting someone, I was totally unaware of why I was doing so. Few people ever realize when they are acting according to their own beliefs and when they are meekly submitting to authority."

Milgram summarized the experiment in his 1974 article "The Perils of Obedience":

> Ordinary people, simply doing their jobs, and without any particular hostility on their part, can become agents in a terrible destructive process. Moreover, even when the destructive effects of their work become patently clear, and they are asked to carry out actions incompatible with fundamental standards of morality, relatively few people have the resources needed to resist authority.[1]

There are countless examples through all of recorded history of this behavior—more recently with the torture and abuse of prisoners at Abu Ghraib prison in Iraq. And we see the same principle at work in *Divergent*, both literally, with Dauntless leadership, and metaphorically, with the rest of Dauntless. For Max, Eric, and the other Dauntless leaders

---

[1] For further readings on this subject, I recommend Phillip Zimbardo's book *The Lucifer Effect: Understanding How Good People Turn Evil*.

aware of Jeanine's plans, the massacre of Abnegation is just a matter of following orders; they are able to shift responsibility to their Erudite masters and say, "I was just doing my job." For the rest of Dauntless, the serum administered to them takes away any and all culpability for their actions. People like Christina and Will literally have no choice other than to do their "jobs."

Put another way, Dauntless plays the role of the willing "Teacher" in Erudite's "experiment."

There's really no one thing that led to the downfall of Dauntless, and in turn the downfall of the entire faction system. In aviation, there is a popular model of accident causation called the Swiss Cheese Model, otherwise known as the Cumulative Act Effect. In this model, an organization's defenses against failure are depicted as a series of barriers, represented as slices of cheese. The holes in the slices represent weaknesses in individual parts of the system. As long as any weaknesses (e.g., lack of proper civilian oversight, lack of purpose, a 50 percent attrition rate) vary in their size and position across the "slices," the organization's defenses will still hold. The system fails when the holes in each slice momentarily align, permitting "a trajectory of accident opportunity." In other words, no one of these issues with Dauntless would have caused its downfall, but all of them together certainly did.

By not being given a real purpose or proper civilian oversight, Dauntless was set up to fail by the very organization that wanted it to succeed. For all their knowledge about genetics, when the Bureau of Genetic Welfare forced segregation into factions, yet had no crossfaction oversight, they failed to take into account basic human nature that is encoded in all of us at the deepest levels. We need a purpose and we need each other.

Janine K. Spendlove is a KC-130 pilot in the United States Marine Corps. In the science fiction and fantasy world she is primarily known for her best-selling trilogy, War of the Seasons. She is also the cofounder of GeekGirlsRun, a community for geek girls (and guys) who just want to run, share, have fun, and encourage each other. A graduate of Brigham Young University, Janine loves pugs and enjoys knitting, making costumes, playing Beatles tunes on her guitar, and spending time with her family. She resides with her family in Washington, DC. If she had to pick a faction, she'd go to Dauntless and look to shake things up a bit. Find out more about Janine at JanineSpendlove.com.

On the surface, Allegiant *feels like a radical departure from* Divergent *and* Insurgent. *Most of the characters are the same, but they're in an entirely new place, dealing with new knowledge and new situations. The relationship between* Allegiant *and the rest of the trilogy isn't so much about the plot—though of course the events at the Bureau directly affect the fate of the city. Rather, the relationship is thematic, as Tris and her small group of Allegiant find themselves confronting the same issues of control and societal upheaval they thought they'd left back in Chicago.*

The events of Allegiant *reflect earlier events in a number of ways, but the clearest narrative echoes are between the factionless and the fringe. Here, Elizabeth Wein traces the role of the factionless over the course of the trilogy, and looks at what they and their fringe counterparts have to say about how change happens, in* Divergent's *world and in our own.*

EMERGENT

The Rise of the Factionless

ELIZABETH WEIN

I find it really hard not to think of the factionless as a kind of sixth faction in the Divergent trilogy. *Emergent* would be a good name for them if they were going to have a faction identity—though of course the whole point of their existence is that they *don't* identify with any faction. As the Divergent trilogy opens, the factionless are the underprivileged outcasts of faction society. Over the course of the trilogy, they become the revolutionaries who want to lead the way to a new world. Their path is riddled with violence and good intentions gone awry, and their attempt to reform society gives us a painful insight into the nature of revolution.

My dictionary defines "emerge" as "to rise from an obscure or inferior position." Something that is "emergent" arises unexpectedly; one of its synonyms is "urgent." It's the root of the noun *emergency*, which suggests panic and urgency when you hear it, although there's nothing in the word "emerge" that evokes these connotations.

Nor is there any indication, in the beginning of *Divergent*, of how uncontrollable the emergent factionless will become by the end of the trilogy. They are presented early on as the downtrodden of the world of Tris' ruined city, the homeless without a face. They scare Tris in the vague way the homeless scare the middle class in our own world: she doesn't like the way they look or smell, but she's really more afraid of sharing their fate than of what they might actually do to her.

In the first book we never see anything that leads us to believe there is anything more complex to this down-and-out level of society. When *Divergent* opens, the first time Tris mentions the factionless is when she describes the area in which they live. Tris is more familiar with the factionless than she'd like to be because the Abnegation live in close proximity to them: the Abnegation have purposefully decided that part of their mission of selflessness is to provide for the factionless.

The area where the factionless live, according to Tris in *Divergent*, is a place of collapsed roads, stinking sewer systems, dumped trash, and empty subways (we don't learn until *Allegiant* that this destruction was heaped on them from outside when an uprising was quelled by the United States government). Tris tells us the factionless have to do "the work no one else wants to do. They are janitors and construction workers and garbage collectors; they make fabric and operate trains and drive buses. In return for their work they get food and clothing, but, as my mother says, not enough of either."

This information is just *loaded* with contradictions, which should tip us off right away that there's more to the factionless than Tris realizes. The factionless are described as doing the "work no one else wants to do," but the work Tris describes them doing is absolutely necessary to a functional society—city life, even in a half-inhabited ruin, would grind to a halt without janitors and construction workers and garbage collectors. Tris says they "make fabric," yet they have to be given clothing—why don't they make their own clothing out of the fabric they produce, even if they have to steal it? And what's so terrible about being a bus driver?

The willing reader, sympathizing with Tris, may find it easy to ignore these holes in her understanding of the factionless. But we need to remember that she is still quite ignorant of them at this point. Her mother is more closely, though still (Tris believes) indirectly, linked to them—"she organizes workers to help the factionless with food and shelter and job opportunities." Tris' first encounter with one of the factionless takes place early in *Divergent*, when she has to pass a factionless man on a street corner. She stares at him, which encourages him to ask her for a food handout. When she offers him a bag of dried apples, instead of taking them, his behavior becomes threatening: he grabs her wrist, makes a suggestive remark, and insults her— but then his aggressive manner falls away and as he takes the apples, he warns her to choose her faction wisely.

We don't learn much about the factionless in *Divergent* that's not filtered through Tris' deeply suspicious and fairly uninformed viewpoint. The factionless beggar's evident poverty and threatening actions are what Tris expects from him—it's almost as if he's playing along with her expectations. But then he does the unexpected and gives her advice. It's *good* advice, too—*"Choose wisely."* Perhaps the man is speaking with regret of his own choices. (It's also, for Tris, advice that is loaded with irony. The one thing she doesn't want to choose, of course, is *wisdom*, the wisdom of the Erudite.) Already in this scene, the description of the factionless that Tris gives us undermines her own stereotype of what she expects the factionless to be.

We get intriguing hints about the factionless throughout *Divergent*, but we're never told anything in detail. Tris tells us her mother once baked banana-flavored bread with walnuts for the factionless, but Tris herself is never allowed to taste such "extravagant" food until she enters the Dauntless compound. Will reminds the other Dauntless initiates that Dauntless police "used to patrol the factionless sector," and Tris points out that her father was "one of the people who voted to get the Dauntless out." His stated reason was that the poor don't need policing, but given the close ties hinted at between Abnegation and the factionless, could there be more to it than that? Words like "patrol" and "police" are our first hints that the factionless might turn out to be a fighting force to be reckoned with.

When the new Dauntless initiates' families visit the faction transfers in *Divergent*, Cara, Will's older sister, shows Erudite prejudice against Abnegation by accusing Tris' mother of using her factionless charity agency for the purpose of "hoarding goods to distribute to your own faction." When we meet Jeanine in person during her attempt to control the city, she also connects the factionless and Abnegation, telling Tris that both the factionless and Abnegation are "a drain on our resources." Jeanine intends that the Erudite should get rid of both of them.

Although these few vaguely damning assessments of the factionless amount to *everything* we know about them by the end of *Divergent*, it is clear that they are going to be a source of unrest. However, it's not yet obvious that they're going to sow the seeds of revolution.

The next glimpse we get of the factionless isn't until nearly a fifth of the way through *Insurgent*, when Tris, Caleb, Tobias, and Susan leave the Amity compound to return to the city. Their group gets on an unlit moving train only to discover that it is full of factionless—all of them armed, one with a gun. Tris wonders where the gun comes from, but their other weapons are homegrown—a bread knife and a plank of wood with a nail sticking out of it.

Now, for the first time, we get a good look at some of these people. In the darkness, Tris is able to make out that their tattered clothes are a collection of faction colors: one man is wearing "a black [Dauntless] T-shirt with a torn [gray] Abnegation jacket over it, blue jeans mended with red thread, brown boots. All faction clothing is represented in the group before me: black Candor pants paired with black Dauntless shirts, yellow [Amity] dresses with blue [Erudite] sweatshirts over them." Tris assumes the clothes are stolen, but that's showing her learned prejudice about the factionless; there's no reason to believe these clothes aren't just handouts or rejects, or even purposefully created disguises. Also, though Tris doesn't know it yet, there is a large Divergent population among the factionless, which is subtly foreshadowed in their multicolored clothing.

The man with the gun turns out to be Edward, one of the unsuccessful Dauntless initiates from Tris' own group. And this simple fact makes the encounter so much more intense. It's no longer one group of desperate strangers confronting another: it becomes a conflict between people who know each other. Their potentially conflicting purposes are bound together, and this bond is pulled tight when Tobias tells the factionless group his name—Tobias Eaton—and is recognized by them in turn.

Now, finally, the reader gets to see how the factionless really live and gets a glimpse of who they really are. Like the homeless of our own world, these people are in fact just ordinary people who have fallen on hard times. The connection between Tris' life and that of the factionless is emphasized in the way she actually recognizes the battered buildings and fallen streetlights as she enters the factionless neighborhood—this isn't new territory for her. This is the way she used to walk to school, the landscape of her childhood, familiar.

Deeper into the factionless sector, the street stinks of garbage, rats scamper among piles of trash and rubble, and when Tris and her group finally enter a building the windows are so grimy that they don't allow light to pass through. The interior is like a refugee shelter: a communal space where people of all ages cook, eat, live, and sleep. They chat and tell stories; children are playing. When they eat, they pass food from hand to hand, everyone sharing from the same pot or can. The sense of unity and loyalty is striking, nor is it lost on Tris. She realizes, for the first time, that "the factionless, who are supposed to be scattered, isolated, and without community . . . are together . . . like a *faction*."

Edward explains that they've been a coherent group for some time—in fact, since Abnegation started supplying them with food, clothes, and tools. But another, bigger shock about the factionless awaits Tris—the fact that Tobias' mother, Evelyn, whose funeral Tris herself attended, is alive and leading them. So the rumors do have foundation—there is a movement astir among the factionless not just to take control of their own fate, but of that of the greater faction society in which they live. They are *emergent*.

Evelyn's organized. Her office is hung with maps detailing Divergent populations and factionless safe houses. The safe houses communicate by painting coded messages on billboards—"Codes formed out of personal informtion—so-and-so's favorite color, someone else's childhood pet"—and I can't help thinking of the radio codes sent from free London to Resistance groups in Nazi-occupied Europe doing exactly the same thing. The factionless are now revealed as a resistance group, both a grassroots and a guerrilla organization. But painting pictures on billboards is a slow, difficult means of communication; Caleb comments that "news takes a while to travel among the factionless." They lack the technology and the resources that are available to their enemies.

Evelyn reveals that the factionless have the highest population of Divergent in the city. Though neither Tris nor the reader knows it yet, what this actually means is that the factionless have the highest population of genetically healed people in the city. Being factionless is one of the things that saves many of the Divergent, for Jeanine mistakenly believes them to be largely among the Abnegation, whom she mostly succeeds in destroying. In opposition to Jeanine's plot, the goal of the factionless is to overthrow Erudite, to "establish a new society. One without factions."

During Tris' first real encounter with the factionless, Edward explains to her that most of them are from Dauntless, "then Erudite, then Candor, then a handful of Amity." Very few Abnegation become factionless during initiation, so their only representation is those few who survive the simulation attack at the end of *Divergent*; Susan reveals that there is a large group of Abnegation members living in one of the factionless safe houses. It's fair to say that the Chicago factionless at the end of *Insurgent* represent all factions, in addition to the Divergent—they are an integrated population.

Evelyn convinces Tobias to attempt to merge the loyal Dauntless (those who haven't joined Jeanine) in an alliance with the remaining factionless population. Evelyn knows there will be "destruction" involved in her coming revolution, and she hopes the Dauntless will be able to provide her followers with much-needed weapons and skills. Her terms are conditional—she wants to ensure that the factionless are allowed a place in the resulting government and are given full control of Erudite data, which they intend to destroy.

In the meantime, the factionless continue their traditional dependence on Abnegation, using Abnegation housing—an improvement on "cardboard boxes that contain frayed blankets and stained pillows"—even though the remaining Abnegation, under the leadership of Tobias' father, are staying well out of their way. The scene of happy camaraderie that greets Tris when she stays in Tobias' house before the battle against Erudite is like something in a dream for her—here in a house hauntingly similar to the one where she spent her austere childhood, there is music and laughter and card games, people sharing food and sofas, people touching each other for comfort without being self-conscious about it.

"This is not what I was taught to expect of factionlessness," Tris thinks. "I was taught that it was worse than death."

But did she ever really believe that? Maybe in her heart

of hearts she knew that what she'd been taught was a load of propaganda. She's easily led, but good at sniffing out truth. While she's still a schoolgirl, before she chooses her own faction, Tris states that for herself and her peers "our worst fear, greater even than the fear of death [is] to be factionless." It's a fear that's programmed into her. She is reminded of this at the Choosing Ceremony when Marcus tells the initiates, "Apart from [the factions], we would not survive." Yet obviously, the factionless *do* survive, even before Evelyn becomes their leader.

The most telling indicator that being factionless is *not* everybody's worst fear is that the factionless—or becoming factionless—isn't a feature of any fear landscape we see in the trilogy. Tris has *got* to realize that the work the factionless do is not necessarily life threatening or soul destroying: that driving a bus or a train is a learned skill, not a punishment; that garbage has to be collected on a regular, organized basis, and it doesn't have to be the work of slave labor; that these less-attractive contributions to society are in fact vital to civilization (no one in Tris' Chicago would ever get *anywhere* without that reliable, punctual, frequent, free metropolitan rail service, which continues to run on time at all hours of the day and night throughout the entire faction war).

The lesson Tris learns in *Insurgent* is that "[The factionless] are not characterized by a particular virtue. They claim all colors, all activities, all virtues, and all flaws as their own." Of course this is also true of the Divergent, like Tris, who are capable of a limitless range of emotions and talents. Tris, too, can claim all virtues and flaws as her own. She can claim responsibility for her own actions.

The planned alliance between Dauntless and the factionless is threatened when Tobias agrees to betray all the factionless safe houses to spare Tris from Jeanine's torture—a risky breach in the battle lines, which is only saved by the fact that some of them have already left the safe houses and that there are more Divergent among the factionless than Jeanine realizes. A subtler flaw in this alliance, which Evelyn surely doesn't take into account, is that Tris doesn't really believe in it. She's concerned about the aftermath of the destruction of Erudite, which she—and most other people, since it's in the Faction History textbook—see as an "essential" faction, since they provide all of society's medical care and information technology. Even though Tris has now seen the factionless for herself, has experienced their doctoring and witnessed their adaptability and mechanical aptitude (they recondition abandoned motor vehicles, among other things)—and even though Tris is Divergent herself—she's still so much a product of the faction system that she doubts her world can survive without it. Her concerns "spill out" as she explains to Johanna, in their moonlit meeting at the Amity compound, "The Dauntless have allied with the factionless, and they plan to destroy all of Erudite, leaving us without one of the two essential factions. I tell her that there is important information in the Erudite compound . . . that especially needs to be recovered." For a faction transfer and a Divergent with aptitude for three different factions, Tris is astonishingly loyal to the system in which she's grown up.

But more than that, Tris is loyal to her parents. The fact that her parents died trying to protect the Erudite data from destruction is a strong motivation for her to want to protect it as well. Tris' devotion to her family is always the deciding factor for her, overriding all her other loyalties.

So there are a number of issues affecting Tris' decision

to leave the factionless and become "Insurgent," as Fernando labels the small band of rebels who want to make sure the Erudite records are not destroyed. Fernando defines an "Insurgent" as "a person who acts in opposition to the established authority, who is not necessarily regarded as belligerent." Tris, who is willing and able to fight if she has to, does not like to see people get hurt, and her instinct about the misguided tactics of the factionless is right on target. As the factionless take over Dauntless weapons, in the manner of so many revolutionaries before them, they prove uncontrollably violent in rebellion.

Evelyn, as the leader of the factionless, has rightly guessed that those who call themselves "Insurgent" are too conditioned to the faction system to allow it to fall apart. It is neither battle nor negotiation that convinces Tris a new way forward might be necessary; it takes a message from *outside*—the recording made by Edith Prior—to wake Tris up to the fact that there might actually be a higher power *outside the fence* pulling the strings of her world.

By the end of *Insurgent* and the beginning of *Allegiant*, the emergent factionless have embraced their identity as a cohesive group, which is inherently a kind of faction of its own. Now they have designed their own symbol, an empty circle, which they wear proudly. They become armed vigilantes, prowling the streets of Chicago and shooting or beating up anyone wearing a faction symbol. They issue orders for existing faction members to mix their color-coded clothing; no more than four members of any faction are allowed to live together in the same building. Gone is the caring group dynamic Tris witnessed in Tobias' house; card games have been replaced with riotous violence. "Death to the factions!" is the battle cry of the factionless.

Poor Evelyn—she'd really like the revolution to be a success. She's a pure communist at heart. Obsessed with rules, she tries to organize jobs on a rotation basis, with a united society in which every member makes an equal contribution to the life of the city. She is able to stop the chaos in Erudite headquarters at the close of *Insurgent* with a few commands. But she is perceived to be a tyrant and a dictator by those fighting against her, and when she's not on the scene her factionless rabble are all too willing to take matters into their own hands. Their bloodthirst is heartbreakingly illustrated in their unprovoked attack on the Candor boy who they claim is violating the "dress code." They hold public trials for traitors but make the trials private when the verdict is "obvious." Their "emergent" status has indeed evolved into an "emergency."

However, the factionless are not the only group capable of revolution in the world of the Divergent trilogy. *Equality*, and the need for change when a society fails to treat its members fairly, seems to be an issue that is unlimited by faction boundaries, personality differences, or genetic mutations. Not surprisingly, the inequalities of the factionless military dictatorship inspire yet another rebellion: that of the Allegiant— those who are loyal to the faction system, similar to Tris' small band of Insurgent in the previous book. So it's no surprise that Tris becomes Allegiant herself. But though both groups share a common loyalty to the faction system, Allegiant represents faction loyalty with a difference. The Allegiant want to help the Divergent among them. And so a group of them leave the city and finally discover the world outside the fence. This is where they will find the answers to the questions Edith Prior's video raised, the ability to change, and the true solution to all their societal issues.

Veronica Roth does a very daring thing as the author of this trilogy—she feeds us information through Tris' limited understanding for two entire books, making the reader wait with bated breath for the saga to continue until we are able to find out the bigger picture. In the world of *Divergent* and *Insurgent*, the limited landscape of the fenced-in city is all we know, all anyone knows, and there are so many questions that the reader can ask about this world: Where does the steady supply of electricity and water come from? Where do material supplies come from—dishes, medicine, computers, watches, furniture, railway cars? How come the trains *always* run on time?

Not until the third book do we get the revelation of the puppeteers behind the puppet show and realize that Tris' sheltered life in faction society has left her incredibly naïve as to how a functional society is supposed to work. When Zoe tells her about the uniforms for support staff in the Bureau of Genetic Welfare, Tris' first reaction is that these people must be like the factionless simply because they're doing jobs no one else wants to do. Zoe corrects her gently: "Everyone does what they can . . . Everyone is valued and important." But again, Tris' instincts are dead on target. Just because these people are "valued and important" doesn't mean they're not segregated. There is a class difference at work here, too—the difference between the genetically pure and the genetically damaged.

Tris recognizes the unfairness of the situation even before she knows the reason for it, just as she recognizes that the fringe occupies the marginal position in outside-the-fence society that the factionless occupied inside-the-fence. Tris has an eye for spotting society's dispossessed. She's shocked by the torn clothes and desperate sleeping conditions of those living outside government society, worries about how the fringe copes during winter weather, and is amazed and proud to discover that her mother's background is so rooted in the very life she finds so appalling.

There are some important differences between the fringe and the factionless, however. For one thing, the fringe's territory is huge, stretching between Chicago and Milwaukee. But the truly significant difference is that while the factionless are society's outcasts, many of those who inhabit the fringe have *chosen* to live outside society. The fringe have actively rejected the system; the factionless were rejected *by* it. By their very nature the people of the fringe are revolutionaries. It is a slower and more subtle revolution than the armed resistance of the factionless, and one that continues to thrive despite occasional doses of memory serum administered by the government when they attempt raids outside their territory.

Tris' mother, in her journey from fringe vagrant to government mole in Dauntless to Abnegation charity worker, is a shining example of how quiet persistence can also be a form of revolution. In fact, the fringe, like the factionless, could also be described as *emergent*, as its members rise from obscurity and inferiority to become key players in the reform of society.

In the final showdown in factionless headquarters— formerly Erudite headquarters—when Tobias goes to confront Evelyn, the gun-toting, unreasonable, faceless factionless are given a face and voice in Grace, a former Abnegation member Tobias recognizes from his childhood. It is Grace who leads Tobias to meet Evelyn. She carries a gun now, unthinkable for Abnegation. But she is not using it for mindless violence. She is defending herself. Seeing her, Tobias recognizes that the Abnegation were "just as broken as the other factions." Grace, who in defending herself has broken away from her Abnegation roots, reminds the reader through her personal growth of what Tris and her companions are really trying to achieve: a peaceful solution in which individuals are able to live in harmony on their own terms.

The world of the Divergent trilogy is often a world of stark contrasts: the black and white of Candor; the jump-or-die lifestyle of the Dauntless; the irrevocable choice at the age of sixteen to leave your family forever. There is no room here for hesitation, no room for *diversity*. The factionless, who embrace the Divergent and wear the colors of all factions, bring about the beginnings of revolution. But as a group they're only able to see the violent side of revolution. You can't change a society just by holding it at gunpoint. Reflection, tolerance, organization, and patience are also necessary ingredients for change.

This is where the role of the individual comes into play: Natalie, devoting her life to change from within; Tris, whose act of sacrifice makes it possible for a new society to emerge; Tobias, willing to negotiate with the mother who allowed him to be abused and then abandoned him; and ultimately, the heroic and tragic Evelyn, who nobly backs down in the end. She disbands her army of factionless, but she also suggests—indeed, *demands*—as part of her final terms that those who stay on in the city should *vote* on their leaders and social system. Through Evelyn, the factionless arrive at a democratic new society. The changes we see in the factionless of the Divergent trilogy seem to tell us that true revolution can only be brought about through the actions of clear-sighted individual leaders who are willing to take into account the voice of the people—emergent.

Elizabeth Wein *is the author of* Rose Under Fire *and* Code Name Verity, *which was voted number one by teen readers in the Young Adult Library Services Association Teens Top Ten list for 2013. Thirty-two thousand teen readers took part in the voting. She'd say she was Abnegation, but she's proud of that! Elizabeth is also the author of The Lion Hunters cycle, set in Arthurian Britain and sixth-century Ethiopia. Originally from Pennsylvania, she has lived in Scotland for over fourteen years. She is married and has two teenage children. Her daughter Sara suggested the topic for this essay.*

ACKNOWLEDGMENTS

For their assistance with the manuscript, the publisher would like to thank the following:

Soetkin Charlier and Faiza Zainab Khan
at The Divergent (thedivergent.net)

Megan Caristi at The Divergent Lexicon
(divergentlexicon.com)

Jessi Iuraduri and Adam Spunberg
at TheFandom.Net

ABOUT THE EDITOR

Leah Wilson *is Editor-in-Chief of Smart Pop Books and the editor of* The Girl Who Was on Fire: Your Favorite Authors on Suzanne Collins' Hunger Games Trilogy, *among other titles. She has a BA in Culture and Modern Fiction from Duke University, and lives in Cambridge, Massachusetts.*

Her aptitude quizzes keep coming back Abnegation, despite her deep appreciation for bright colors, laughter, learning, and cake.

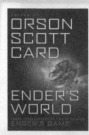